SCRUTINIZE

MISSION MEMORY ENHANCERS

SCRUTINIZE

MISSION MEMORY ENHANCERS

SUJATHA RENGANATHAN

INKFEATHERS PUBLISHING
www.inkfeathers.com

CONTENT CURATION PARTNER

mugafi

Contents

Chapter 1

Congratulations SP Vikram

A shiny white Innova with the word "police" printed on it smoothly glided into the parking lot of the Commissioner of Police's office amidst the bustling Monday morning rush. Mr. Vikram Krishnan, the Superintendent of Police, happily parked his vehicle in front of the building and confidently approached the entrance, ready to tackle the challenges of the day. With his unwavering focus and dedication to public safety, Mr. Vikram Krishnan sets a shining example for his staff and the community at large.

Miss Reena Tripathi, the receptionist, warmly greeted Vikram amidst the constant buzzing of ringing phones.

"Hello, Miss Tripathi. Is the commissioner available?" Vikram inquired in a casual tone.

"Good morning, sir. He has an appointment with the collector," Reena replied.

"Alright. Just let me know once he's back in the office," Vikram added as he proceeded inside.

Suddenly, Vikram's phone rang. Vinod Patil, his inspector, was on the line.

"Hi, Vinod," Vikram answered.

"Good morning, sir. Have you arrived at the office?" Vinod asked.

"Yes, Vinod. Is Mr. George with you?" Vikram inquired.

"Sir, we'll be there in a minute," Vinod assured him.

"Okay. Meet me in the conference room," Vikram responded.

"Yes, sir. We'll see you there," Vinod said before hanging up the phone.

Vikram instructed a police officer to gather all the officers and lead them to the conference room. The room was filled with high-ranking officials eagerly awaiting the arrival of Inspector Vinod Patil and Mr. Michael George, a superintendent from the London Police.

As Vinod and George entered the crowded room, Vikram stood up to greet them and warmly shook hands with Mr. George.

"Welcome, Mr. George. It's an honour to have you here. We sincerely appreciate your collaboration in our efforts," Vikram remarked.

Vikram enthusiastically introduced George to his team. "Please give a warm welcome to Mr. Michael George, the Chief Superintendent of the UK Police. He played a crucial role in dismantling the notorious global mafia gang alongside our Indian Police," he proudly announced.

The room erupted into applause and cheers, showing their admiration for Vikram and George's remarkable achievements.

Mr. George's cheeks slightly blushed at the enthusiastic response, and he humbly replied, "Wow, I am truly touched by your kindness. I extend my heartfelt gratitude to Vikram and his dedicated team for their invaluable support in dismantling the multinational malicious network of the mafia gang."

I'd love to share the whole story and how it unfolded, Vikram said with a big smile. He began narrating the sequence of events, and a sense of calm spread among the officers as they listened attentively.

Dr. Manisha Gupta, a 55-year-old general practitioner, was in charge of a small hospital with limited beds, an intensive care unit (ICU), an ICCU, and an operating room. The hospital's capacity to treat patients was enhanced by the regular visits of specialists.

On a Monday morning, Dr. Manisha Gupta, the Chief Doctor of Get-Well Hospital, visited Vikram to seek assistance. Vikram politely welcomed her to his office and offered her a seat.

Good morning, sir, began. I'm Dr. Manisha Gupta, the chief doctor at Getwell Hospital.

Taking a deep breath, Dr. Manisha expressed her concerns. "Sir, last Friday, we faced a truly terrifying situation."

A 17-year-old girl was urgently brought to our hospital in cardiac arrest at around 9:00-9:30 p.m.

"Oh, my God!" exclaimed Vikram, his concern evident in his voice.

"Is she alright?"

"Yes, she is out of danger now. However, I have this nagging feeling that her cardiac arrest was not a mere coincidence," Dr. Manisha confided.

"It does sound suspicious," remarked Vikram, leaning forward to inquire further.

While examining her, the doctor explained, we noticed extensive allergic rashes on her body. This led us to conduct an allergy test.

"You wouldn't believe it, but the test results were alarming," she continued. We found traces of multiple drugs that are typically used under strict medical supervision.

Alarmed, I immediately contacted the girl's parents to inquire if she had been taking any medication They assured me that she hadn't taken any medications in recent days.

Vikram responded, that is quite peculiar. "Do you suspect a drug case?"

Yes, sir, Dr. Manisha affirmed. I need your assistance to investigate.

"Can I meet the girl and her family?" Vikram requested.

"Of course, sir."

She then proceeded to share a similar incident involving a 17-year-old boy named Arjun, who had visited the hospital with his father the previous week.

In addition to a high fever, he was experiencing severe headaches and skin rashes. I prescribed medication and scheduled a follow-up appointment in case his condition worsened.

During the follow-up, we planned to conduct blood tests to determine the cause of his symptoms, Dr. Manisha continued.

Vikram was taken aback. Divya, the girl with the cardiac arrest, had also complained of headaches. Now, she has rashes all over her body, just like Arjun, observed.

"How closely are these two incidents related?" Vikram pondered aloud. "I'm not sure about the extent, but I believe there could be a connection. Can you arrange a visit to find out?" Dr. Manisha gently requested.

"Alright, doctor. I'll come to your hospital within the next 30 minutes to meet Divya and speak with her parents," Vikram replied, adding, make sure Divya's parents are present at the hospital.

Dr. Manisha expressed gratitude and assured him, "Certainly, sir," before leaving his office.

Vikram took the initiative and dialled Inspector Vinod's number.

"Vinod, get ready," Vikram instructed. "We need to go to Getwell Hospital for an investigation."

"Sir, should we leave immediately?" Vinod asked.

"I'll brief you about the details during our half-hour drive. Just find the exact location of the hospital," Vikram instructed. "Yes, Sir, "Vinod acknowledged.

Exiting his office, Vikram joined Vinod in the car, and they headed towards Getwell Hospital. Little did they know that rest would soon be in short supply, and this was just the beginning of a high-speed chase.

Chapter 2

Divya in Coma

Vinod dropped Vikram off at the hospital entrance and went ahead to park the car.

"Hey, morning! I'm SP Vikram Krishnan," said Vikram as he approached the front desk. "I wanna meet your chief doctor, Manisha."

Vinod quickly caught up with him. "Good morning, Sir." Dr. Manisha is eager to meet you. "To get to her cabin, just go straight down this corridor and take a left," the receptionist said.

As they walked, Vikram noticed the cozy size of the facility, while appreciating its great condition. Vinod nodded in agreement. The nameplate on the door read, "Dr. Manisha Gupta, MD, General Medicine."

Just then, a nurse emerged from the room. Vinod introduced himself and explained their reason for being there. The nurse nodded, quickly went into the doctor's cabin to announce their arrival and then allowed them inside.

Dr. Manisha greeted them warmly. "Shall we go meet the patient and her family?"

They took the lift to the second floor and proceeded to the ICCU unit. As they approached, Vikram couldn't help but notice the anxious expressions on people's faces. He witnessed nervous and fearful emotions radiating outside the critical care unit.

They sanitized their hands and put on masks before entering. The room was bustling with medical personnel. Everyone seemed occupied.

Among the elderly patients, a little girl was lying completely still, with a tangle of cables hooked to her tiny body. Vikram asked the doctor, "Any signs of improvement?" "Not much," the doctor added.

"But her pulse is stabilizing. We've brought in Dr. Sandeep, an internal medicine specialist and neurologist, for a second opinion."

Vikram asked Dr. Manisha, "Can we meet her parents?"

Vikram, Vinod, and Dr. Manisha headed to the waiting room, where Divya's terrified parents spotted Dr. Manisha and hurried up to her. "How is our daughter doing, doctor? We have no idea what happened to her," they sobbed.

Dr. Manisha reassured them, "Now her pulse rate is stable. She will slowly come out of the coma too." She then introduced Vikram and Vinod as the superintendent and inspector of police, respectively.

"They want to speak with both of you. Don't be alarmed, it's just a casual inquiry," Dr. Manisha told Divya's parents.

When the police arrived unexpectedly, Sudhir Verma and Shylaja Verma, Divya's parents, along with their neighbors and family friends Jaspal Kaur and Veena Kaur, became concerned.

Vikram introduced himself, "Hi, my name is Vikram Krishnan, Superintendent of Police. You're both Divya's parents, right?"

Sudhir confirmed, "My name is Sudhir Verma, and this is my wife, Shylaja Verma. Meet Jaspal and Veena, our next-door neighbors and friends."

Vikram asked Sudhir, "Could you please tell me what happened on Friday night?" As they started talking, someone spoke from behind and asked, "How is Divya? Is her health better now?" When they turned around, they saw that it was Mr. Ramesh, Sudhir's neighbour.

Vikram inquired about Ramesh because he was interested in the man. Sudhir explained, that Mr. Ramesh works as a research analyst and has a Ph.D. in biotechnology. He often helps high school students in our area with biology and chemistry. He takes classes for them.

Vikram addressed Ramesh, "Mr. Ramesh, you know that visitors aren't allowed in the ICCU, but you could have called Mr. Sudhir and asked about Divya's health."

"Yes, I know that sir, but...," Ramesh replied.

Vikram turned to Dr. Manisha and said," Doctor, I need to talk to Divya's parents alone. Could you arrange a separate room for us? "Dr. Manisha immediately asked the receptionist to arrange a private room for them on the same floor.

Meanwhile, Jaspal and Veena went to the hospital canteen to have some coffee. Ramesh headed towards the elevator. In the private room, it was just Divya's parents, Vikram, and Vinod.

Vikram began the conversation by asking, "Could both of you elaborate on what happened? Do you both work?"

Sudhir replied, "Yes, sir. I work as a manager at a private bank. My wife, Shylaja, is a stay-at-home mom who also works as a freelance Spanish interpreter."

Vikram asked Sudhir, "Could you tell me exactly what happened on Friday night? I want to know more."

Vikram instructed Vinod to record the statement as Sudhir continued describing the events of that fateful evening at their home.

At the restaurant, Jaspal and Veena were discussing why the police had come and why they were being questioned. After finishing their coffee, they walked to the ICCU's waiting room and saw Ramesh speaking to the chief nurse of the ICCU. Jaspal and Veena waited in the corridor for Sudhir and Shylaja.

Chapter 3

Friday 8:30 pm

Vikram and Vinod were ready to listen. Sudhir was about to share the details of what happened on Friday night.

Around 8:30 p.m., Shylaja was busy preparing dinner. Sudhir had just come back home after playing badminton and was greeted by the irresistible aroma coming from the kitchen.

Intrigued, he made his way straight there, exclaiming, "Wow, that smells amazing! I need to get to the kitchen right away!"

Shylaja chuckled and responded, "Oh, it's nothing special, dear."

"You made our daughter's favorite dish?" Sudhir asked. "Where is she? Has she not returned home from her class?"

"I believe she's sleeping," Shylaja guessed. Sudhir looked puzzled. "Without eating?"

"After Ramesh sir's class, she complained of a bad headache," Shylaja explained. "I advised her to rest."

Sudhir replied, "Today, sir made her study more, and that's why she got a headache," and headed towards Divya's room.

"Could you please bring her for dinner?" Shylaja requested.

When Sudhir came back from the kitchen, he cheerfully greeted Divya with, "Hey, Divya, how are you? It's dinnertime. So, what's cooking? Mom prepared your favorite dish!"

Divya emerged from her room with a furrowed brow, moving slowly towards Sudhir.

Sudhir had a sense that something was amiss. "Hey, Divya, what's wrong?" he asked, his expression filled with concern. "You look so pale."

In a panic, he shouted, "Shylaja, come quickly!" Fear filled his voice. "Divya doesn't seem well. We need to take her to a doctor."

Hearing Sudhir's cries for help and seeing Divya clutching his shoulder, Shylaja rushed out of the kitchen.

She was breathless when she reached Sudhir, who was holding Divya still. Shylaja splashed water on her face to revive her, but she showed no signs of waking up.

Feeling the urgency, Shylaja rushed outside and called their neighbour, Veena. "Please come quickly!"

Ramesh, along with Veena and her husband Jaspal, arrived simultaneously and were shocked to find Divya unconscious on the floor.

"Let's take her to the doctor," Ramesh suggested. "I'll grab my car." He walked out without waiting for permission.

"Sudhir, we need to take her to the hospital," Jaspal demanded. Sudhir and Shylaja followed Jaspal closely as he carefully lifted Divya.

Unaware of the severity of the situation, the parents joined the rest in piling into Ramesh's car, while Veena stayed behind.

"Don't worry, Divya will be okay," Ramesh assured everyone. "We'll go to my friend's clinic near Children's Park."

"What are you talking about?" Jaspal questioned sternly.

"You can drive to Getwell Hospital, which is not far away. It's about four or five kilometres from here," Ramesh clarified.

"Can't you see how critical the child's condition is?" Jaspal asked.

"Let's get going to Getwell Hospital."

Veena arrived in her car and drove them to Getwell Hospital.

They reached the hospital quickly.

Divya was quickly brought to the emergency department, with the security personnel at the door urgently requesting a stretcher.

Veena arrived just in time to join the worried group outside. She did her best to calm down Shylaja, who was visibly upset.

"Have you noticed if Divya was dealing with any study-related anxiety or possibly feeling depressed?" Vikram asked Divya's parents. "How is your relationship with her? Have there been any recent conflicts or arguments?"

"Sir, Divya is not the top student in her class, but she excels in both academics and extracurricular activities. She had some typical concerns of a student her age. Of course, like any mother and daughter, we have our fair share of disagreements and conflicts," Shylaja explained.

Vikram probed further, asking, "When did she first complain of a headache?"

"Sir, when I returned home from the market around six in the evening, Divya was completely engrossed in her mobile device," Shylaja recalled. "I asked her if she had returned from class, but she didn't respond.

"And what about today? Did you attend the NEET class?" Shylaja inquired.

"I went to the NEET class and then stopped by Ramesh Sir's house to return a book," Divya explained, "and I just got home."

She quickly returned to her phone. I urged her to hang up and start working, but she retreated to her room and shut the door behind her.

"Then I went to the kitchen to start making dinner," Shylaja explained. She told me about her headache around 7 p.m., and I advised her to take some rest,

Vikram thanked her for her help. Vikram asked Vinod to find Ramesh. Vinod returned and informed Vikram that he couldn't locate Ramesh: "Sir, he's not outside."

Sudhir quickly suggested to Vikram, "If needed, I can give you Ramesh's mobile number." He then provided Vikram with Ramesh's phone number.

Shylaja questioned Vikram, "Sir, could you please explain why you're asking about our daughter?" Vikram gave a detailed explanation, revealing that Dr. Manisha suspected that their daughter's cardiac arrest might not have been natural.

Sudhir and Shylaja were shocked and yelled, 'What? The doctor didn't inform us about this!"

"So, are you implying that we had a hand in harming our daughter?"

Shylaja's anger surged as she spoke. "Please don't misunderstand," Vikram reassured them. "We're simply investigating Dr. Manisha's suspicion. It doesn't mean you're under suspicion; it's just a standard procedure."

"Sir, Divya is everything to us. We would never do anything to harm her," they vehemently claimed. Sudhir shouted in desperation. Sudhir and Shylaja walked out of the room together, seeking solace in each other's company.

"Ramesh, it's SP Vikram," Vikram spoke on the phone. "I got your number from Sudhir."

"Sir, yes, how can I assist you?" Ramesh politely responded.

"Join us in the room; we need to talk," Vikram replied.

Without wasting any time, Ramesh hurried to the elevator and made his way to the room.

Chapter 4

Anxious Dr. Prasad

The house is cozy and warm. A white Hyundai Creta slowed down in front of the gate and honked impatiently. Even though he was watering the plants, the worker quickly unlocked the gate.

As Dr. Prasad hastily parked his car and entered his house, Nirmala, his wife, hurriedly left the kitchen in fear of the noise. "What's wrong, dear?" she asked.

"Not now, Nirmala!" Dr. Prasad responded curtly, clearly in a bad mood. Nirmala remained silent as he walked to his room and threw his belongings onto the sofa.

He paused for a moment before entering. "Nimmi," he said to his wife, "Babu and Kumar are planning to come over for a meeting later. Please prepare lunch for them." Nirmala realized she shouldn't ask any more questions and nodded.

Dr. Prasad rushed to freshen up and get dressed before meeting his childhood friends, Babu and Kumar. He had established his clinic as a doctor and, like many others in his profession, desired fame and fortune.

While he was getting ready, let's learn more about Prasad, Babu, and Kumar's past. They had all attended the same elementary school. Babu had the highest grades among them. Both Prasad and

Babu aspired to become doctors.

Babu didn't have enough money to pursue a medical course, so he chose to major in biological research and went on to get his Ph.D. in the same field. He now works as a scientist and research analyst.

Prasad began practicing medicine after completing his Bachelor of Medicine (MBBS) and Doctor of Medicine (MD) degrees in internal medicine.

Kumar currently ran his own successful pharmaceutical business after earning his master's degree in pharmacy.

As Prasad waited in the living room, his worried expression was evident. He heard a car door slam shut, catching his attention.

Prasad was about to open the door when Kumar walked in. They sat down on the couch and anxiously waited for Babu.

Kumar could tell that Prasad was uncomfortable with just a glance.

"Did Babu inform you of when he'll arrive?" Kumar asked.

Prasad interrupted and said, "He called me early this morning and said that the previous trial cannot be repeated."

"He told me to wait until he gave me the go-ahead to act."

"Oh no, why do we have to redo the trial?" Kumar exclaimed.

"I'm just waiting for him to understand what I mean. We don't have much time left, and we need both the study paper and a complete trial report for the conference in London," Prasad said, his voice strained.

"I'll try to reach him," Kumar said, dialling Babu's number. He hung up in disappointment when no one answered.

Prasad kept saying, "Babu seems to have lost sight of our shared ambition to complete this research and make progress."

After contemplating what was happening, Prasad asked himself, "Why is this happening? I had everything planned out, but things aren't going as expected."

"I considered getting the research paper and trial records from Babu and flying to London myself to submit them, which would have been beneficial. Later, I could come up with a story to explain why the application didn't work."

"I wouldn't have any trouble assuring Kumar that I can secure contracts for his pharmaceutical company to manufacture drugs. He'd be thrilled," Prasad thought.

Prasad wrestled with his thoughts, "How can I make the most out of both of them, though?"

"To prevent anyone from finding me afterward, I would have assumed a new identity."

"Calm down, Prasad. Don't worry, everything will be fine," Kumar reassured him, feeling stressed himself. Prasad remained silent, contemplating different ideas in his mind.

Chapter 5

Investigation—Mission Divya

"What do you think about this case?" Vikram asked Vinod. "From your perspective, do you think her heart attack was natural?"

"No, sir, Vinod responded. That girl's heart attack was unusual. We need to investigate further. Something triggered the attack."

Vikram added, "It happened recently. There must be a clue somewhere. It's worth considering."

Their conversation was interrupted by a knock on the door. Vinod opened the door, and Ramesh entered the room.

Vikram gestured for Ramesh to have a seat. Vinod prepared to record the conversation.

Vikram asked, "What do you do for a living?" "I'm a research scientist," Ramesh replied.

"How did you first meet Divya and her family?" Vikram inquired.

"Divya used to come to my place for chemistry and biology study sessions," Ramesh answered.

"Do you offer tutoring for specific subjects?" Vikram asked. "Oh, please don't call it tutoring," Ramesh said. "Children in the community come to me with a thirst for knowledge."

"Do you provide free classes?' Vikram asked.

"No," Ramesh replied. "I believe in fair pricing. All the money I earn goes to a non-profit organization that supports underprivileged children's education.

"I'm surprised. Why are we discussing this? I'm here to inquire about Divya's health," Ramesh said.

"Don't worry, stay calm," Vikram reassured him.

"Can you remember when you first met Divya?"

"I've been helping Divya with her studies for the past two years," Ramesh explained.

"We're just neighbors." He added, "Not as close as the Jaspals though."

Vikram continued, "According to Divya's mother, Divya started experiencing headaches after your classes. Are you an extremely strict teacher?"

Ramesh spoke softly. "Sir, the children in the community enjoy spending time with me because I am an easy-going educator."

"If you want to know more about me, you can talk to the kids in the community," Ramesh suggested.

"Speaking of Divya, she is a diligent student. She enjoys exploring and learning new things," Ramesh said. Ramesh continued, "However, I have the impression that her parents put a lot of pressure on her academics."

Ramesh further added, "They are quite strict with her because they want her to have a strong work ethic, excel in school, and be precise. It might be making Divya unhappy."

"Sir, the way her parents have treated her must have negatively impacted her mental health," Ramesh expressed his concern. "May I share something with you?" Ramesh said.

"Divya and Kunal were often seen hanging out together at coffee shops. I don't think he's the right person for her.

"Who is Kunal?' Vikram asked.

Ramesh replied, 'They go to the same school, but he doesn't perform well academically.

"Can I leave now?' Ramesh asked.

Vikram directed Vinod to gather more information about Ramesh.

"You should not leave the city," Vikram told Ramesh.

"Thank you for your cooperation. If you have any concerns, please let us know, and we will do our best to assist you. We might need to call you back if necessary."

Vinod began collecting Ramesh's address, phone number, and other contact details.

Ramesh stood up and walked away without saying anything.

"Should I approach the Punjabi couple for questioning?" Vinod asked.

"Let's talk to Dr. Manisha again before we reach out to them, so we have a complete understanding of Divya's situation," Vikram suggested.

"We need to confirm her availability," Vinod stated.

Vinod called the receptionist to check if Dr. Manisha's outpatient department (OPD) hours had ended and informed them of their desire to meet with her.

"Sir, it will take an additional hour," the receptionist informed.

"Should I call the Punjabi couple?" Vinod asked.

Vikram nodded in agreement.

He got up and went to find Veena and Jaspal.

Chapter 6

Furious Ramesh

Ramesh felt like he was being accused, so he stormed out of the room. Divya's parents, Sudhir and Shylaja, were filled with worry and pain as Jaspal and Veena tried to calm them down.

Ramesh pointed at Sudhir and yelled, "Your wife told the police it's my fault that your daughter is in this condition. How can she blame me?"

Everyone was shocked. Shylaja quickly clarified, "Hold on, we didn't blame anyone. I just shared what I knew."

Frustrated, Shylaja said, "We don't understand why the police are involved in our daughter's health problems."

To try to calm things down, Sudhir explained, "Ramesh, we were trying to reach out to Dr. Manisha to get more information about Divya, but the police got in the way."

Ramesh retaliated, "Maybe Divya is so stressed out because of both of you." The couple was too shocked to respond.

This angered Jaspal, so he said, "It's not just you; the police are also investigating us. We're equally clueless."

Ramesh's attitude upset Veena, and she muttered, "He clearly doesn't understand the gravity of the situation."

Ramesh gave her a mean look and stormed off. Vinod naively asked, "Did Ramesh storm off angrily?"

Veena breathed a sigh of relief and replied, "Yes, he misunderstood our interaction with the police as a false accusation."

Sudhir, perplexed, said, "What's going on exactly?"

"All we can gather is that Ramesh lost his composure," Shylaja suggested.

As soon as she heard this, she proposed, "We should get some clarification from Dr. Manisha."

Vinod advised them to wait until they saw Dr. Manisha. He turned to Jaspal and said, "Hey Jaspal, Vikram sir wants to talk to you and your wife."

Jaspal agreed, and the three of them went to the room where Vikram was sitting, leaving Shylaja and Sudhir waiting outside.

When Jaspal met Vikram, he asked, "Sir, what's going on? Why are we being interrogated?" "Our main concern is Divya, she's unconscious,"

Vikram reassured Jaspal before inquiring about their relationship with Sudhir and his family.

Veena replied, "We have been a part of their lives since Divya was born seventeen years ago. We're like family."

Veena expressed her deep concern and insisted, "Their entire family is happy. Please refrain from making unnecessary assumptions about that girl."

Vikram, not having any information at the moment, told them that he would discuss it with Dr. Manisha later. He thanked them for their cooperation and care and asked for their patience.

Jaspal and Veena thanked Vikram and Vinod and left the room. Vinod and Vikram headed to the elevator to meet Dr. Manisha.

Sudhir, anxious for answers, caught up with them at that point.

Vikram assured Sudhir that he would keep him updated after the appointment with Dr. Manisha.

Sudhir urged Shylaja, Jaspal, and Veena to join them in meeting Dr. Manisha along with the police officers, to find out why she had involved the police and what exactly happened to their daughter.

All three agreed with Sudhir and walked towards the elevator, uncertain of the shocking information that awaited them as they met Dr. Manisha.

Chapter 7

The Trios Meet

It was already past noon, around 1:10 pm, when Babu casually strolled into Prasad's house, tossed his car keys onto the couch, and made a beeline for the fridge. Opening it up, he greedily took a swig from a bottle of ice-cold water.

Prasad and Kumar observed Babu's refreshment session as he settled comfortably on the couch. Giving Babu a moment to compose himself.

Prasad exclaimed with a grin, "Hey, guys! I've got some fantastic news!" Both Babu and Kumar leaned in, eager to hear what Prasad had to share.

Rising to his feet, Prasad announced, "Our research has been recognized and accepted by the committee. They're now asking for the trial reports of our invention."

"That calls for a celebration!" Kumar exclaimed, enveloping Prasad in a tight hug.

"It's fantastic to hear that our idea is getting recognition," added Babu.

However, Prasad couldn't help but notice that Babu seemed preoccupied. Curiosity got the better of him and he inquired, "What's on your mind right now, Babu?"

Babu hesitated for a moment before replying, "We still have a lot more work to do in our research. Let's hold off on celebrating just yet."

Prasad reassured him, "When I said "over," I meant we have more time to finish it. Plus, these trial reports will pave the way for us to attend the Medical Forum meeting in London."

"I'm looking forward to that day," chimed in Kumar. Babu advised Kumar, "Hang in there a little longer."

Then, addressing both his colleagues, Babu implored, "Please have patience; I've already mentioned what we need to do. Let's wait until the final trial."

Prasad was eager to turn their research paper into a profitable venture as quickly as possible. He wanted to ensure that nothing went wrong and that they could sell it for a good price.

"I think if we explain the situation, they'll understand," Prasad reassured Babu. "After all, the committee is already aware of our idea."

Worried about the financial stakes, Kumar expressed his concerns, "You both should know that I've invested a lot of money into this research. It's too important for me to lose."

"No need to worry, Kumar. We'll submit our results, get them approved, and not only will we not lose any money, but we might even make a substantial profit," Babu said to calm Kumar.

Following that, Babu suggested, "You know what, Prasad? It might be a good idea to keep the important research documents at either your house or the company office."

"Should I send my driver to retrieve the papers?" Dr. Prasad asked.

"Yes, I" 'll give you a call, and then you can send your driver over,' Babu replied.

Babu then grabbed his keys from the couch and left the house. The distant purr of his car's engine, which signalled his departure, gradually faded away into silence.

While they were alone, Kumar asked Prasad, "Do you think he'll complete the trial?" "Either he has to finish it by tonight, or we'll need to make alternative plans," Prasad remarked.

"Will you join me?" Prasad asked Kumar. "Of course, Prasad," Kumar replied.

Kumar continued with concern, "Listen, I've established a dedicated research unit in my pharmaceutical company for this project. I'm paying a considerable amount to the analysts who are working on the research, and I've also invested a significant sum of money into it."

"We can't just sit back and wait," Prasad concluded their conversation. "Remember, Kumar, I've got this project. We'll keep moving forward, even if he decides to quit because this is an international endeavor,"

Prasad emphasized. Later, the two decided to grab some food to satisfy their hunger.

Chapter 8

Dr. Manisha

The clock at Getwell Hospital struck one. However, Dr. Manisha was busy seeing patients in the OPD.

After finishing her consultations, Dr. Manisha had about thirty minutes to catch up with her receptionist, head nurse, and other hospital staff. Once her OPD round was complete,

she made calls to the ICU and other ward heads to ensure everything was running smoothly. Shortly after, the receptionist informed her that SP Vikram, Divya's parents, and other guests were waiting to meet her.

Without wasting any time, she invited them in and asked Dr. Sandeep to join her. The room felt tense as everyone took their seats, even Dr. Sandeep and Dr. Manisha.

Sudhir broke the silence by asking the doctor about Divya's medical case, questioning whether the police had been involved and if there were any suspicions of a crime, like attempted suicide.

Dr. Manisha reassured everyone, saying it was not what they thought, and asked for a chance to explain. She then posed a hypothetical scenario to Sudhir, asking how he would have responded if she had told him that Divya had used drugs.

Shylaja, Divya's mother, stood up in anger and asked for

suggestions from the doctor on how to prevent such damaging things from happening to her daughter. Sudhir stepped forward to comfort her, while Veena and Jaspal offered their support.

As tension filled the room, everyone anxiously awaited Dr. Manisha's update on Divya's health. Dr. Manisha clarified, saying, "I didn't mean to imply that she was a drug user, but her situation is even more critical."

Before Vikram could ask his question, Dr. Sandeep interjected, "Vikram sir, let Dr. Manisha finish discussing Divya's health before you ask your questions." Vikram agreed, saying, "That makes sense, doctor."

Dr. Manisha began by explaining, "When Divya was brought to the hospital, the emergency doctors immediately took her to the ICCU due to the severity of her condition. They started treatment and informed me about it."

She continued, "During those difficult moments, I reached out to Dr. Sandeep for assistance." Dr. Manisha went on to describe the challenges they faced, saying,

"Bringing her back from cardiac arrest was a daunting task. We had to use an automated external defibrillator (AED) to restore her heartbeat to normal. Unfortunately, she lost consciousness and slipped into a coma."

"It was heartbreaking to see a vibrant 17-year-old girl lying there motionless. We had no clue what had suddenly happened," said Dr. Manisha.

She added, "Things took a turn for the worse when she developed skin rashes. It seemed like one complication after another. From cardiac arrest to rashes, it was a puzzling situation." Dr. Manisha emphasized, "Given the circumstances, I ordered a comprehensive set of blood tests, including an allergy screening, and made expediting the results a top priority."

Finally, Dr. Manisha asked, "You have witnessed firsthand how myself, my team of doctors, and nurses have worked tirelessly to bring Divya back to a stable condition." Divya's parents and the others present listened attentively to the doctor's explanations.

Dr. Manisha continued, "I immediately requested a meeting with a cardiologist to examine her. His analysis revealed that Divya's cardiac arrest was not typical. He advised us to closely monitor all potential factors and offered assistance if needed."

Additionally, we had the support of Dr. Sandeep, a renowned neurologist who provides consultations at our hospital. His involvement in treating Divya's coma was crucial,' mentioned Dr. Manisha, suggesting that Dr. Sandeep should share more about Divya's condition.

Dr. Sandeep proceeded to explain the current state of Divya's health and the ongoing treatment. Throughout this challenging ordeal, Shylaja struggled to hold back her tears. Finally, she broke the silence and burst into tears, seeking comfort from Sudhir.

Dr. Manisha paused and then resumed, "While our staff nurse was drawing blood for the tests, she noticed a needle mark on Divya's hand and immediately informed me." Dr. Manisha turned to Shylaja and asked, "Shylaja, do you recall my question regarding whether Divya had recently undergone any blood tests?"

"Yes, doctor, I remember," Shylaja replied with a nod. "I told you that no blood tests had been conducted recently." Manisha continued, "We were astounded when we received the report on Saturday. The presence of a controlled substance in Divya's blood may have caused the cardiac arrest, leading to her coma."

Upon hearing the news of Divya's health condition, shock rippled through the room. Sudhir slumped into a chair, while Shylaja began sobbing uncontrollably. In a distressed voice, she cried out to the doctor, "No, doctor! This cannot be true! My little girl doesn't use drugs. Oh God, what is happening?"

Veena approached Shylaja, holding her hand, and reassured her, "Hey, we know our child. Somewhere, there must have been a mistake. Don't lose hope. She will be alright."

"Doctor, this is unbelievable! How is Divya doing now?" Vikram asked Dr. Manisha.

Sudhir stood in front of Dr. Manisha, hands folded, and pleaded,

"Please, save our daughter."

Sudhir's voice trembled with sadness as he said, "My daughter is terrified of needles, so how could she have received a drug injection?" Tears filled his eyes as he spoke. Jaspal reached out to Sudhir, offering comfort.

Dr. Sandeep reassured them, saying, "Sir, please don't worry about the treatment. We're closely monitoring her condition and administering necessary medication through an IV drip to eliminate the drugs from her body. She will also recover from the coma soon."

Sudhir turned to Vikram and said, "Sir, please record my complaint and find the person responsible for injecting drugs into her."

Shylaja took hold of Dr. Manisha's hand and expressed her gratitude, saying, "Thank you so much, doctor. I have witnessed the dedication and hard work of your efficient team of doctors and nurses in saving my daughter's life. You didn't stop there; you also helped by filing a complaint with the police to find the culprit."

Vikram assured everyone, saying, "I promise you all, I will soon uncover the person behind this medical scam." Vikram turned to Dr. Manisha and asked, "Can you provide me with the details of the boy who had a similar problem as Divya?"

Dr. Manisha called the receptionist and requested, "Please get me the details of Arjun, the patient who recently visited our hospital."

The receptionist arrived at the cabin with Arjun's details within a few minutes. Dr. Manisha handed it over to SP Vikram, who thanked her before leaving the cabin with Vinod.

Before leaving, Shylaja turned to Dr. Manisha and pleaded, "Please save my daughter. You are our guardian angel." Dr. Manisha gently held her hand and said, "Don't worry, she will recover soon. Let's also keep her in our prayers."

Sudhir comforted Shylaja as she continued to cry, and the four of them walked to the waiting room of the ICCU ward.

Chapter 9

Mission Divya Starts

Vikram turned to Vinod and said, "Hey, it's lunchtime. Let's grab a bite and then figure out our next moves."

They made their way to the hospital canteen, which was bustling with activity. People chatted and were having their meals in a clean and lively space. Finding a spot beneath a whirring fan, Vinod ordered a mini meal. While waiting for their food, Vikram took out his phone and attempted to call the commissioner of police. However, his number was busy, so Vikram decided to try again later.

As they waited for their meals, Vinod asked, "Sir, how should we approach this case? Should we consider it a drug-related incident?"

Vikram pondered the question and replied, "Not exactly a drugs case. Perhaps we should classify it as a medical scam." Before proceeding any further, we need to inform the commissioner and seek his permission to proceed. "Let me first talk to the commissioner, explain the situation, and obtain his approval."

Their meals arrived, and they started to eat. Within a few minutes, they finished their meal, settled the bill, and headed out. Vikram made another attempt to contact the commissioner.

This time, the commissioner answered the phone and greeted Vikram, saying, "Ah, Vikram. What's the matter?"

"I need to discuss a medical case with you, sir. May I provide you with a briefing?" Vikram asked respectfully.

The commissioner permitted Vikram to proceed with the briefing. Vikram proceeded to describe the case in more detail, sharing the information provided by Dr. Manisha about Divya.

The commissioner posed the question to Vikram, asking, "Should we treat this as a drug case?"

Vikram responded with a nod and replied, "Yeah, we got some clues, but let's tread carefully here. We're dealing with a 17-year-old girl," said Vikram. His aim was to wrap up this case quickly.

After hearing Vikram's response, the commissioner gave him the go-ahead and asked, "Who's assisting you with this case?" Vikram replied, "Sir, Vinod has joined me, and soon Subhash and a few constables will be part of the investigation process."

Vikram and Vinod walked out of the canteen and hopped into their vehicle. Vikram checked the time and said, "It's already 2:30 PM. Let's kick off our investigation at Divya's school."

"Vinod, give Sudhir a call and gather details about the school." Vinod promptly dialled Sudhir's number and extracted information about the school and its schedule.

He then contacted the school office, introduced him, and politely informed them about their visit to meet the principal. He also rang Inspector Subhash and instructed him to meet them at Divya's school along with his team.

Vinod queried, "Sir, who should we focus on during this investigation?" Based on the current circumstances, Vikram mentioned that they should meet Divya's class teacher and principal, as well as her friends Kunal, Arjun, and Ramesh.

As they journeyed along the bustling road towards Divya's school, Vikram turned to Vinod and said, "We need to expedite our inquiries so that we can make progress and solve the case swiftly."

When they arrived at the school, Inspector Subhash and the constables eagerly awaited their arrival. Subhash and the constables saluted Vikram. Vikram instructed Vinod to brief Subhash and the constables about the case and assign them tasks that would aid in an early resolution.

While Vinod, Subhash, and the constables delved into a discussion about the case, Vikram strolled towards the school office. Meanwhile, Vinod assigned two constables the responsibility of monitoring Ramesh and Sudhir's residences and reporting any suspicious activities.

He directed two other officers to keep a close eye on Divya's parents and ensure her safety at Getwell Hospital. Vinod provided Subhash with the residential address of Arjun and said, "Subhash, go and visit them. I'll give you further instructions after that."

Once his tasks were completed, Vinod leisurely made his way towards the playground. As he observed the children playing football, he couldn't help but admire their dedication and hard work. He eagerly anticipated the conclusion of Vikram's meeting with the principal.

Chapter 10

Investigation at the School

Vikram made his way towards the school's reception, casually greeting the receptionist, "Hey, good morning! I'm Vikram, the Superintendent of Police. Is your principal available? I need to talk to her about a case."

The receptionist smiled and replied, "Sure, take a seat in the lobby, I'll check if she's free and let you know." Vikram nodded, saying, "Thanks!" The receptionist warmly responded, "You're welcome, sir."

Meanwhile, in her office, the principal was informed by the receptionist about Vikram's visit. She asked if he could be sent in. As Vikram waited in the lobby, his attention was drawn to a glass shelf displaying medals, shields, and trophies.

Time flew by, and as the school bell rang at 3:30 PM, indicating the end of the day, Vikram noticed the teachers dutifully ensuring the school grounds were calm and orderly. Soon after, the receptionist informed Vikram, "Sir, you may proceed to meet the principal now."

Vikram thanked her and lightly knocked on the door before entering when granted permission. Inside the principal's office, two other teachers were present alongside the principal. Vikram greeted the room, "Good morning, Madam. I'm SP Vikram. I want to inquire about one of your students, Divya, who's in the 12th grade."

The principal gestured to Vikram, "Please have a seat, sir. We just received information about Divya this morning. I have asked her class teacher to meet with her parents and gather more details about her health."

Vikram briefly explained the case to the principal and emphasized the need for their assistance in understanding Divya's situation. The principal contacted Divya's class teacher, Radhika, through the intercom and requested her presence. Shortly after, Radhika arrived. "Radhika," the principal addressed her, "this is Mr. Vikram, the Superintendent of Police.

He is here to gather more information about Divya, who seems to be in trouble." Radhika turned to Vikram and greeted him, "Good afternoon, sir. How can I assist you?" Vikram didn't waste any time and asked, "What can you tell me about Divya's class?"

Radhika responded promptly, "Sir, Divya is an outstanding student. She is friendly and well-behaved, and nobody has ever complained about her. Her academic performance is equally impressive."

Vikram expressed his gratitude to the principal, saying, "Thank you for your cooperation, Madam." The principal replied, "Sir, it's our duty. We hope the case gets resolved quickly, and the person responsible is held accountable. We will pray for Divya's swift recovery and return to school."

Vikram thanked her once again before leaving the room. As Vikram exited the principal's office, he met Vinod. Sensing Vikram's urgency, Vinod inquired, "Sir, what did the school say about Divya?" Vikram relayed the information shared by Divya's class teacher,

"Divya is an excellent and responsible student. There are no concerns about her behavior and character. She has consistently achieved good grades."

Vinod updated Vikram on the progress made by Inspector Subhash and the constables. Impressed, Vikram commended him, "Well done, Vinod. You have expedited the investigation."

Vinod expressed his gratitude and continued, "Sir, I have some information about Kunal. He also resides in Sunshine Colony, just like Divya." It was evening, around 4:15 PM, when Vikram instructed Vinod, "Drive to the Sunshine Colony." During their journey, Vinod's phone rang. It was a call from Subhash, and Vinod activated the speakerphone.

Vikram inquired, "Hi, Subhash. Did you manage to meet Arjun?" Subhash responded, "Yes, sir. I located Arjun's residence, but it appears that he and his father went to Getwell Hospital for a check-up.

Arjun had a severe headache last night." Vikram expressed his appreciation, "Thank you, Subhash. Proceed to the hospital. We will rendezvous with you once we complete another investigation."

Vikram dialled Dr. Manisha's number and informed her, "Doctor, we heard that Arjun was admitted to your hospital due to severe headaches. Please keep him there, and we will arrive shortly to question him."

Dr. Manisha assured Vikram, "Let me verify, sir. If Arjun is here, we will ensure that he is available for you to speak with." Vikram thanked Dr. Manisha and planned to visit the Sunshine Colony to meet Kunal and gather more information about Divya.

Chapter 11

Doubt...Doubt

In the waiting room of the ICCU ward, all four of them anxiously await news of Divya's return from her coma. Shylaja entered the ICCU ward, hoping to catch a glimpse of her daughter. Unfortunately, she couldn't see her.

As she approached, Sudhir sat beside her, holding her hand, and she whispered, "I want to see our daughter." Sudhir squeezed her hand tightly and reassured her, "Don t worry. I'll ask the nurse for permission to visit Divya."

Sudhir glanced at the clock—it was already 4 p.m. He walked to the chief nurse's cabin and joined Jaspal.

The nurse was busy checking reports, so Sudhir and Jaspal waited patiently in front of her. Sudhir politely asked, "Excuse me, Sister. We have a small request. We'd like to see our daughter, Divya, who is admitted to the ICCU ward. We haven't seen her all day."

The chief nurse replied, "Sir, the chief doctor has instructed us not to allow visitors inside the ICCU ward. However, considering your condition, I can permit only the parents to see her for five minutes." Jaspal responded, "Don't worry, sister. Only Divya's parents will go and visit her, and we'll follow all the protocols to enter the ICCU ward."

Sudhir thanked the chief nurse and went to inform Shylaja. The chief nurse instructed the duty nurse to accompany them to see Divya. The duty nurse provided them with face masks and sanitized topcoats as they entered the Intensive Critical Care Unit (ICCU) ward.

Shylaja and Sudhir cautiously entered the ICCU room. Their hearts sank when they saw their daughter connected to various machines and wires. Whispering to Sudhir, Shylaja said, "It breaks my heart to see our daughter in this room surrounded by elderly patients." As tears welled up in Shylaja's eyes, Sudhir held her hand tightly and comforted her as they approached Divya's bedside.

Overwhelmed by emotions, they couldn't suppress their tears, and they wept silently together.

"Please keep the noise down," the duty nurse calmly told them. "I understand how you feel seeing your daughter in this condition. Just remember that there are other critical patients in this room." Sudhir apologized to the nurse, and they both moved closer to Divya.

Shylaja gently placed her hand on her daughter's forehead, her voice filled with love and concern. "Sweetheart, what's happened to you? Come on, my love, open your eyes and talk to us. What's all this talk about you? Divya, please wake up, look at us, and let's go home."

They stood by their daughter's side, silently watching her for a few minutes. The nurse then returned and asked them to leave the ICCU room. With heavy hearts, both Sudhir and Shylaja reluctantly left the ICCU ward.

As they stepped outside, Sudhir turned to Shylaja and softly said, "Shylu, do you remember how vibrant and full of life Divya used to be?" His voice carried a tinge of sadness as he spoke to Shylaja.

Once outside, Shylaja couldn't hold back her tears. Veena offered her comfort and support. Amidst her sobs, Shylaja told Veena, "You know how lively and joyful Divya has always been, right? It's unbearable to see her lying there like a lifeless flower. With numerous wires and tubes connected to her frail body, she looks so pale."

"Who could have given such a deadly drug to our daughter, Divya?" Jaspal asked with concern. "It's like poison. What kind of person would do this? How could this happen?" Jaspal's questions echoed the queries of everyone present.

Shylaja agreed, "Yes, bhaiya, it's possible that she had no idea what was going on. Hey Shylu, try to remember," Veena urged before questioning, "Where did she go recently without you or Sudhir Ji?"

Shylaja pondered for a moment before responding, "She didn't deviate from her usual routine. She attended her regular NEET coaching classes, just like the other students. She only meets her friends on weekends."

Sudhir had a thought, "Shylu, you mentioned that she went to see Ramesh to find some answers. Did she go by herself?" Sudhir wondered.

Shylaja explained, "I wasn't home on Friday evening. I went to the market and returned at 6:45 p.m. I asked her what she was doing, and she told me that she went to return some books to Ramesh's house after her NEET class. "

"That's when I found out she was there. Around 7:30 PM, she started complaining of a headache." Curiously, Jaspal asked Sudhir, "Sudhir ji, isn't Ramesh a research analyst?" Sudhir confirmed, "Yes, he is. He visits a few colleges and universities as a visiting professor and teaches in his field."

Jaspal expressed his suspicion, "Could he be the one who gave her the drug?" "Oh my God!" Shylaja and Veena exclaimed simultaneously. Veena shared her observations of Ramesh's strange behavior earlier that morning, particularly when he yelled at Shylaja for revealing something to the police.

"Yes, Veena, you're right. He was alone and seemed to be having a continuous conversation with the duty nurse at that time. But we didn't question him; our main concern was Divya,"

Shylaja added, with Jaspal agreeing with Veena's insights. Jaspal suggested to Sudhir, "Sudhir, let's speak to the nurse to find out if she's still on duty and what Ramesh was discussing with her."

Agreeing with Jaspal's idea, Sudhir and Jaspal went to the nurse's cabin. To their relief, the nurse who had been taking care of Divya on Friday night was still there.

Sudhir told Jaspal, "Alright, let's find her and get answers to our doubts." Once they located the nurse in the nurse's cabin, they politely approached her.

Sudhir said, "Excuse me, nurse. We apologize for the interruption. We just need a few minutes of your time." The nurse responded, "I have a moment to spare for you. What can I do for you?"

Sudhir continued, "I'm sorry to bother you. We have a question regarding my daughter Divya who is currently in the ICCU room." The nurse informed them, "Her condition hasn't changed, I'm afraid. She is still unconscious."

Jaspal then interjected, "Sister, we just need a few additional details." Sudhir inquired, "After Divya was taken to the ICCU on Friday night, a man approached you and started conversing with you. Do you recall what he was discussing?"

"Oh, indeed, how could I forget him?" the nurse replied after a brief pause. "Why are you interested in knowing?" Sudhir explained, "We're just trying to understand his concern for my daughter."

"I was occupied with taking care of your daughter in the ICCU, where the medical situation was constantly changing," the nurse explained, pausing briefly before continuing.

"But he kept inquiring about the treatment and whether she had regained consciousness. His constant questioning began to irritate me. I gave him a stern look and warned him that I would report him to our head doctor if he didn't stop."

"After that, he left me alone." Jaspal suggested, "I'm not sure what his intentions are. We should inform SP Vikram, sir."

Afterward, they approached Shylaja and Veena and shared the details provided by the nurse. Sudhir took out his phone and dialled SP Vikram's number. Unfortunately, it went to voicemail. Sudhir decided to send a message, expressing their concerns about their daughter's health condition and their desire to discuss it further.

Chapter 12

Investigating Kunal

In the afternoon, around 4:30 p.m., the Innova pulled up to Sunshine Colony. Vinod used Google Maps to find his way to Kunal's place.

"Sir," Vinod said to Vikram, "I think this is the coffee shop Ramesh mentioned where Divya, Kunal, and their other buddies hang out." The coffee shop was on the way to Sunshine Colony.

Vikram replied, "Vinod, let's grab some coffee and start our investigation, man."

They hopped out of Vinod's car and walked into the coffee shop together. Vinod ordered two cappuccinos.

The place was buzzing with teenagers. Vikram noticed it as Vinod placed the order. Vikram introduced himself and struck up a conversation with one of the staff members.

"Hey, when do you guys get super busy? Seems like a lot of teens hit up this spot," Vikram asked.

"Sir, we welcome everyone here," the staff replied. "Teens, adults, all sorts of people come and chill out, here" After they finished their coffee, they left the cafe.

"Sir," Vinod said, "Sudhir left a voicemail for you," Vikram told

Vinod to play it. After listening to the message, Vikram asked Vinod to call Sudhir.

Vinod made the call to Sudhir. Sudhir answered, saying, "Hello sir, have you heard the voicemail?" Vikram replied, "Yeah, Sudhir, tell me what important info I need to know."

Sudhir informed Vikram about their concerns and asked him to include their doubts in the investigation.

"Alright, Sudhir, I'll treat this as your complaint and take the necessary action," Vikram assured.

"By the way, what do you think about Kunal?" Vikram asked Sudhir.

Sudhir questioned Vikram, "Kunal? Why do you need to know about him? He and Divya were best friends since they were kids."

"Sudhir, we're in Sunshine Colony right now," Vikram revealed. "We're planning to visit his house to gather more info about Divya and her crew."

"Kunal and his parents are like our extended family, sir," Sudhir said. "So, please, be easy on them. They're good people. Sir."

"Sudhir," Vikram said. "We got to talk to everyone who knew or is connected to Divya to figure out what went down. It's crucial for the case."

Vikram and Vinod drove through Divya and Ramesh's place to get to Kunal's house. When they reached, Vinod rang the doorbell and a woman quickly opened it. Vinod introduced them and explained the purpose of their visit.

Kunal's mother welcomed them, asked them to take a seat, and called Kunal and his dad. Kunal and his dad emerged from their rooms as Vinod said, "Sir, meet SP Vikram and I am Inspector Vinod. We're here to find out more about Divya. We've heard she's good friends with your son."

"Divya is like our daughter to us," Kunal's mother said. "We can't believe she had a heart attack and is unconscious now. We've known Divya since she was a little girl,"

Kunal's dad continued. "Kunal and Divya go to the same school," Kunal's dad added. "They know each other well. Our families, the Jaspal family, our family, and Sudhir's family, are all close within this community. "

I called Jaspal to see if they needed any help. My wife and I will go to the hospital to give them a break.' But Jaspal shared some shocking news - traces of drug-equivalent medicine were found in Divya's blood sample.

Both Kunal and his mom were taken aback and shouted, "What?" In a fierce tone, Kunal asked Vikram, "Do you think she is using drugs?" Kunal's eyes filled with tears as he said, "Sir, it's highly unlikely that Divya is a drug user. She's a good and helpful friend."

"Could I call Anu and our friends? They'll vouch for her and testify that she would never use drugs." Kunal pleaded. As Kunal's mother consoled him, Vikram said, "Kunal, we're here to learn more about Divya, and who better to talk about her than her friends? That's why we need your help and support."

Vikram continued, "We didn't say she had taken any drugs; there are traces of medicine that are similar to drugs. Don't worry, just tell us everything you know about Divya."

Kunal began sharing about their friendship. "We've been friends since kindergarten. We were classmates until 10th grade. In 11th grade, I joined the business group, while she opted for the science group."

"Within this neighbourhood, Anu, Divya, Charan, Pradeep, and I are all close friends. We used to hang out at each other's houses, at the park, and sometimes at the coffee shop on the corner of our street," Kunal explained.

Vikram asked Kunal, "We heard she goes to Mr. Ramesh for classes." "Yes, she does," Kunal replied. "Sometimes she goes to Ramesh Sir's place for chemistry and biology classes to clear her doubts. Anu also goes with her. And she never goes anywhere alone."

Vikram noticed a change in tone and asked, "What caused the change when Ramesh was mentioned? We've heard that the kids at Sunshine Colony like him."

'Sir, he dislikes some of us because we make noise and play cricket in the field behind his house. He sees us as troublemakers who don't study," Kunal responded.

"We were talking outside the coffee shop on Wednesday after class. Divya and Anu liked to take rounds on my scooter. Ramesh Sir looked at us as if we had kidnapped the girls," Kunal said.

Vikram thanked Kunal's parents, stood up, and walked over to Kunal. 'Thank you, Kunal," he said. "Sir, my friends and I are willing to help if you need us," Kunal offered.

"We hope you'll bring us some good news soon." Vikram and Vinod left the house after expressing their gratitude to the family.

Chapter 13

Kunal and Friends

Kunal quickly rushed to his room, snatched his phone, and sent an urgent message to the group, "Let's meet at the coffee shop in 10 minutes. It's really important, I have some major news to share about Divya."

Kunal anxiously awaited the responses from his friends as he stared at his phone. The replies started pouring in, with everyone using the thumbs-up symbol to signal their agreement.

As he left the room, Kunal informed his mother, "Hey Maa, I'm heading to the café to meet my friends." His mother curiously asked, "Why? What's the matter?" Kunal replied, "I need to discuss the police visit and share some important updates about Divya's health with them."

In response, his mother revealed, "Your dad and I are going to the hospital to see Divya and meet Sudhir Ji and Shylaja." With his Activa key in hand, Kunal hopped on his scooter and made his way to the coffee shop. Standing outside the café, he anxiously awaited the arrival of his friends.

As Anu arrived at the café first, she immediately bombarded Kunal with questions, "Hey Kunal, how is Divya? Did you go to the hospital or did your mom and dad visit her?"

Sensing her curiosity, Kunal responded, "Hold on Anu, let's wait for Charan and Pradeep. I promise you, what I have to say will shock all of us just like it did to me. I'm still reeling from it."

While Kunal was engrossed in conversation with Anu, Charan, and Pradeep sprinted down the street to join them. "Alright guys," Kunal continued, "let's find a quiet spot away from any distractions or disturbances."

Charan immediately suggested, "Why don't we go to the amphitheatre? It's empty and secluded." Following Charan's suggestion, they all made their way to the amphitheatre. Anu, visibly anxious, told Kunal, "I'm scared of the shocking news you're about to reveal."

Seated on the top steps of the amphitheatre, Kunal began recounting the harrowing events of the police visit and the shocking revelation about Divya's condition.

"Can you believe it, guys?" Charan exclaimed, his voice filled with amazement and shock, "They found traces of drugs in Divya's blood." Pradeep, struggling to comprehend the situation, said, "I can't wrap my head around this. How is it even possible? First, a cardiac arrest, then a coma—it's all too much."

Anu, her voice trembling with emotion, cried out, "Divya is not someone who would do drugs. She was always with people, whether in class, at home, or with us." Kunal interjected, "And that crazy Mr. Ramesh dared to label us as bad people, not worthy of friendship."

"Did the police question him too?" Charan inquired. Kunal nodded and continued, "Yes, they also interrogated Divya's parents, Uncle Jaspal, Aunt Veena, and Mr. Ramesh."

Seeking answers, Pradeep questioned, "But why? Who tipped off the police?" Kunal proceeded to enlighten his friends, "You all know that Divya is currently at Getwel Hospital. The chief doctor, Manisha, raised concerns about her condition, suspecting that

Divya's heart attack was not a typical one."

"Upon receiving the report, SP Mr. Vikram and Inspector Vinod went to the hospital to take action," Kunal continued. "They spoke to people in the hospital who were acquainted with Divya, conducting inquiries. Mr. Ramesh was also present at the hospital, where he too faced questioning."

Pradeep interjected, "So, Kunal, why did you gather us here? Is it just to share this information?" Kunal replied firmly, "No, there's more to it. We need to uncover the truth behind Divya's coma and assist the police in apprehending the person responsible."

At that moment, Kunal noticed Anu was lost in thought. Curiosity getting the better of him, he inquired, "Hey Anu, what's on your mind?" Anu hesitated before responding, "I was wondering about how, when, and where the culprit might have administered the drugs to Divya."

"I highly doubt she would have done it to herself." Charan, recalling a particular incident, addressed Anu, "You were with Divya when the three of us went to play football last Friday after our café meeting."

"What was she up to?" Anu explained, "Divya had to return a book to Mr. Ramesh, so she went to his house." "Alone?" Kunal and Pradeep simultaneously questioned, expressing their surprise.

"You always accompany her." Anu clarified, "I had to leave early for a family event, which is why I couldn't go with her." Charan added, "That night, she experienced all the problems and had to be rushed to the hospital."

Kunal voiced his doubts, stating, "Mr. Ramesh may be somehow connected to Divya's condition. It stands out as the only instance where she was alone before complaining of headaches."

Anu pondered aloud, "How can we confirm our suspicions? Should we confront him directly?" Pradeep cautioned, "Ramesh sir won't give us any answers. If he's involved, he'll escape and hide."

Kunal proposed an alternative approach, 'Let's not confront him directly. Instead, we should engage him in a conversation about Divya and observe any changes in his behavior. Anu, you'll have to do it, and the rest of us will be there to support you. We know he doesn't like the three of us.' Unanimously, they agreed to proceed, and thus, they made their way to Ramesh's house.

Chapter 14

Come Let's Visit Ramesh

Vikram instructed Vinod to halt the car after driving the Innova for a short distance. Stepping out of the vehicle, Vikram began strolling, and Vinod quickly joined him. They stopped near a bustling park, observing the lively scene of moms chatting while their children played and raced around.

Some kids cruised along the bike path on their bicycles, while elderly folks engaged in conversation on the park bench. A quaint little shop sold refreshing drinks, cookies, and comforting soups. As the clock struck 6 p.m., the park was teeming with people.

Vinod was questioned about their request to keep an eye on Ramesh's house. Curious, he wondered, where have they disappeared? Vinod replied, Sir, Subhash has already provided me with the information.

You may want to avert your gaze. Those individuals selling water purifiers over there are our undercover police constables.

The public was inquiring about the water purifiers, completely unaware that these individuals were police officers. Meanwhile, Vinod alerted Vikram to look up, stating, Sir, Kunal is approaching us with his friends.

Kunal pointed towards the two policemen and exclaimed, Hey,

that's Superintendent of Police Mr. Vikram and Inspector Vinod. Upon their arrival, Kunal informed Vikram, Sir, they are also friends of Divya. I was the one who informed them about your investigation. We discussed it, and given the circumstances, we suspect someone else may be involved.

Vikram greeted, "Pleasure to meet you all. Who are your suspicions directed towards, and what is the reason?" Charan reported, "Sir, we have reason to doubt Ramesh sir. Divya went to his house alone to return a book, and later that night she complained of a headache. We believe he would harm her by administering drugs."

Vikram replied, "Gentlemen, Divya was not harmed, but the blood tests revealed traces of a poisonous substance. We must not make assumptions or speculate about anyone." "I will reach out if I require support or information," he acknowledged.

"I understand your concerns, but now allow me to do my job." After expressing gratitude to Vikram, Kunal and his friends departed. "Vinod, I believe we should visit Ramesh's residence to gather more information about him," Vikram suggested.

The undercover officers, disguised as sellers, confirmed that Ramesh was indeed at home. Vikram instructed Vinod to contact Dr. Manisha and inquire if Arjun was present at the hospital. Maintaining surveillance on Ramesh's house, Vikram submitted a progress report to the commissioner.

Upon joining the call, Vinod handed the phone to Vikram who asked Dr. Manisha, "Doctor, has Arjun presented himself at the hospital?" "Yes, sir," she replied. "He came in with respiratory problems and a headache. We conducted several blood tests to assess his condition." "Very well, doctor." Vikram informed her, "Following my ongoing investigation, I will visit the hospital to meet Arjun and his father."

Dr. Manisha informed, "Arjun has been admitted to the hospital as an inpatient, and we have ensured that his father accompanies him. We will closely monitor his health."

"Understood, doctor." Vikram cautioned, "Make sure no one else has access to them or discusses their presence here." Vikram added, "The constables will be dressed in plain clothes to maintain a low profile."

"Alright, sir," the doctor advised them to arrive early. "Vinod, get in touch with Subhash and his team," Vikram instructed Vinod. "We need to proceed to Ramesh's house immediately to gather more information before deciding our next move."

Vinod confirmed, "Subhash and his team will arrive within ten minutes." Vikram and Vinod started walking towards Ramesh's house. Meanwhile, Vinod positioned himself next to the door and rang the bell.

After a short delay, a man in his forties opened the door and inquired, "What do you want?" "We're here to meet Mr. Ramesh. My name is Vikram, and I'm the Superintendent of Police. This is Inspector Vinod," Vikram introduced.

Vikram asked, "Is Ramesh home?" "Good morning, sir. Can you explain your visit to my house?" Ramesh asked skeptically. "We came to inquire about Kunal because our duty demands our undivided attention 24/7. You were the only one who mentioned Kunal to me this morning," Vikram stated.

"On our way back from meeting Kunal, we decided to visit you," Vikram explained. Observing Ramesh's tension, Vikram inquired, "Also, are you living alone? How is your family doing?"

Ramesh replied, "I am divorced, and my former wife left me years ago. Now, Raju, my caretaker, lives with me." Vikram probed further, "Did you mention that you are a scientist or research analyst? If you were a scientist, would you work from home or in a laboratory?"

Angrily, Ramesh retorted, "I work in a research lab outside! Can we get to the point?" "Do you have your research facility, or do you work for a research organization? What is the name of the company?" Vikram pressed on. "Why do you want to know about my job?" Ramesh questioned.

Vikram calmly stated, "It's normal to inquire about someone's profession." "Are you involved in something illegal, or do you work as a detective or secret agent?" Vikram began to suspect Ramesh.

As they were conversing, Inspector Subhash walked in. Furious, Ramesh commented, "This doesn't seem like a routine visit!" Standing up from the couch, Vikram calmly replied, "You're right, Mr. Ramesh. This isn't your ordinary questioning. The situation surrounding Divya seems to lead back to you. Our suspicions compelled us to detain you until we can uncover more about what transpired."

Ramesh demanded, "What are you talking about? As a police officer, you can't say whatever you want." Vikram signalled for Subhash and Vinod to restrain Ramesh. Simultaneously, Vinod apprehended Ramesh while Subhash silenced and handcuffed him. At the same time, a constable handcuffed the caretaker and led him away. The caretaker inquired, "Sir, why am I being arrested too?" Vinod instructed, "Remain quiet. We also need to question you."

Vikram directed, "Take them to our investigation center and place them in separate rooms. Ensure that no one becomes aware of their arrest. I have a considerable amount of work to attend to. Please follow my instructions and wait; I will join you after completing the crucial tasks."

Ramesh shouted, "Give me my phone! I need to speak to my lawyer and friends. I refuse to leave my home." Vinod calmly responded, "Don't create a scene. You have been arrested and will be interrogated." Vinod and Subhash seized the laptop, cell phone, and portable hard drive from Ramesh's office.

Subsequently, Ramesh, his caretaker, and two additional constables were escorted for security purposes. As Vikram departed for the hospital, he instructed the constables, who were posing as salespeople, to secure the doors and remain vigilant.

Chapter 15

Vikram Meets Arjun

People were still waiting to see the doctor at 8 p.m. As he approached the reception area, he asked the receptionist to inform Dr. Manisha.

Sudhir and Jaspal, who were seated in the waiting area, spotted Vikram and rushed towards him, their faces filled with concern. "Hello sir, what's going on?" Sudhir and Jaspal asked simultaneously. "Have you found the person responsible for injecting my daughter?"

"I'll let you know when the time is right," Vikram offered in a comforting tone. "How is your daughter doing?" "She's still in a coma, sir," Sudhir replied with a hint of sadness.

Interrupting their conversation, the receptionist interjected, "The doctor is waiting for you, sir."

After hearing this, he made his way to the doctor's cabin, where Dr. Manisha and Dr. Sandeep were already present. Together, they proceeded towards Arjun's room. Arjun had been admitted to a private room on the ground floor.

As they walked down the hallway towards his room, Vikram questioned the doctor, "Doctor, you mentioned that you had conducted Arjun's blood test. Do you have the report yet?"

"We're still awaiting the full report. Initially, we specifically requested them to look for any traces of a dangerous drug. The complete report will be sent to us tomorrow," explained Doctor Sandeep.

"What does the report say?" Vikram inquired, his curiosity growing. "Sir," Doctor Sandeep continued, "the report now shows a different trace of medicine in his blood. It appears to be an antinode."

"Antinode?" Vikram questioned, puzzled by the unfamiliar term. Elaborating on his findings, Dr. Sandeep began to explain. "Sir, it seems that Arjun might have been administered a medication that had adverse effects on his body. The antinode was given to counteract those harmful effects. The blood report contains traces of this antinode."

Dr. Manisha said, "Sir, we have no clue what kind of medicine he took, which might have messed him up. Only Arjun and his dad can fill us in."

Everyone went to Arjun's room. The bed was slightly raised, and Arjun was popping his pills. Dr. Manisha asked Arjun, "How're you feeling, Arjun? Are the headaches bothering you? Do you always get them? Which doctor do you see when you ain't feeling well?"

Arjun replied. "Usually, I'm headache-free, but I've had one for the last two weeks. It ain't normal, and it's bugging me. And on top of that, I've got skin rashes and stomach issues."

"No worries, Arjun. We'll take care of all your problems." Dr. Sandeep tried to reassure him. "Just hold on tight. We've got your back."

"Can I have a chat with him?" Vikram asked Doctor. "Is he alright? Will he be able to answer my questions? I'll keep it straightforward."

Later, she told Arjun, "This is SP Vikram. He wants to ask you a few things. Just respond if you understand. If any question makes you uncomfortable or stressed, we'll stop."

"Why are the cops interrogating me?" Arjun inquired. "Is something wrong?" It was his dad who asked Dr. Manisha, "Doctor, everything okay?"

Vikram replied, "It's just a routine question, sir." She'll explain later. "Can we get started?" Vikram then approached Arjun, grabbed his hand, and asked, "Arjun, mind telling me what happened? Why'd you end up in this hospital?"

"Sir," Arjun began, "my dad does odd jobs like house cleaning and gardening at Dr. Prasad's place." "How long has he been working at Dr. Prasad's?" Vikram probed. Arjun replied, "I think it's been around nine or ten years."

He used to work at Dr. Prasad's place. Dr. Prasad was a serious person, but his wife, Madam Doctor, was kind-hearted. "Whenever I visited, she would ask me about my studies and my passions. She has always guided and supported me in my education," he recalled.

"About a month ago, when I went to see my dad at their place, Dr. Prasad called me over. He asked me about my studies and commented on how weak I seemed. It was surprising to hear him talking to me and showing concern. He suggested that I visit his clinic so he could give me supplements to boost my energy."

Vikram asked, "Did you go to the clinic?" "Yes, sir," he replied. Vikram followed up, "Did you go alone?" "No, sir. My dad was with me," Arjun answered.

"Okay, Arjun, tell me, what kind of supplement did Dr. Prasad give you? How is the clinic? How big is it? And how many people were there when you visited?" Vikram inquired.

"Dr. Prasad's clinic is located in Sector 12, right across from the kids' park. It used to be a bungalow-style house, which he converted into a clinic. There's a consultation room and two rooms with four beds each," Arjun explained.

"A nurse and a boy were attending to patients."

"Tell me how he treated you," Vikram asked. "We reached the clinic around 9 a.m. There were no other patients at that time. Dr. Prasad was in the consulting room, talking to someone," Arjun said.

Suddenly, Arjun's dad interjected, "Babu sir, that person Dr. Prasad was talking to is his friend. I've seen him at Dr. Prasad's house."

"Babu, is he also a doctor?" Vikram questioned. "No, sir," Arjun's dad replied. Dr. Manisha, Dr. Sandeep, and Vikram exchanged glances. "Did Dr. Prakash give you the supplement medicine?" Vikram asked.

"Sir, I thought the doctor would prescribe me a supplement pill or tablet," Arjun explained. However, instead of giving me a pill, Dr. Prasad decided to administer an injection and check my blood pressure beforehand.

"Right after the injection, they asked me to rest for 30 minutes," Arjun recounted. "Initially, I felt energized and active, but it didn't last for long. Something felt off after about a week."

It had been a long conversation, and Arjun was exhausted and stressed. He turned to Vikram and asked, "Can I take a short break? After talking for so long, I'm feeling completely drained."

Concerned, Dr. Manisha quickly checked his blood pressure to ensure that the readings were accurate. They turned out to be slightly high. "Please let him rest," Dr. Manisha requested Vikram. "His blood pressure seems to have spiked." Vikram agreed and left the room, waiting outside as the doctors attended to Arjun.

Chapter 16

At Investigation Cell

"Let Arjun rest," Vikram informed Dr. Manisha and Dr. Sandeep. "I have some important work at the office. I'll be back in exactly one hour to proceed with the investigation."

Vikram exited the hospital and headed to the office, where Vinod and Subhash were busy working on their laptops in the investigation cell. "Hey, guys. Have you had dinner? Did the police constable also eat?" Vikram inquired. Vinod replied, "Yes, sir. We've all had our dinner. Have you had yours?" Vikram nodded affirmatively.

"What was Mr. Ramesh and Caretaker Raju up to? Did Ramesh cause any trouble?" Vikram questioned. "Sir, when I went to give him dinner, he tried to hand me his phone so that he could call his friends and his lawyer," Subhash explained.

"We informed him that we couldn't give him anything without your permission." Ramesh was being held in the room where they all gathered. Although there was a camera with a microphone in the room enabling them to see and hear him clearly from outside,

Ramesh remained unaware of what was happening beyond those walls. As Vikram entered the room, he noticed the visible signs of stress on Ramesh. There was a small table and a chair in the room. Then he walked out of the room.

Meanwhile, Vinod asked, "Sir, did you meet Arjun? Is there anything crucial about the case?" "Yes, I did meet Arjun and his father. The case bears similarities to Divya's. However, Arjun mentioned that Dr. Prasad, who is a doctor, administered the medicine, while his friend Babu, who is not a doctor, stayed with him," Vikram revealed.

"Doctor Prasad?" Vinod inquired. "Is he a well-known doctor? Does he work at a hospital or a clinic?" "Arjun mentioned that Prasad's clinic is near the children's park,"

Vinod responded. "Is that the same clinic mentioned by Jaspal in the investigation, which Ramesh intended to take Divya to?" Subhash asked. "There's a possibility that Ramesh may have been aware of Prasad and Babu," Vikram contemplated.

Subhash informed Vikram, "Sir, we noticed frequent calls from a contact named Prasad on Ramesh's phone, along with a few from a person named Kumar. However, we didn't answer those calls."

Vinod interjected, "Another name has come up, Kumar. I'm not sure how many more names will surface. It's currently Prasad, Ramesh, Babu, and Kumar." "I believe these four individuals are connected.

The key link we have so far is the injection, our primary witness," Vikram stated. "It is important to understand their motives. Through Arjun's father, I obtained Prasad's home and clinic addresses. I have informed the local inspector, Mr. Sunil, to send police constables to keep watch over Prasad's residence and clinic,"

Vikram explained. He proceeded to call Dr. Manisha to inquire about Arjun's condition and to request permission to continue the investigation. He emphasized the significance of Arjun's testimony in unravelling the secret puzzle.

Dr. Manisha assured Vikram, "Arjun is in a much better state now compared to when he arrived at the hospital. Please proceed with your investigation." Vikram instructed Subhash, "You stay in the office.

Vinod and I will go to Getwell Hospital to continue the investigation with Arjun, and then we'll proceed to Ramesh's house. We'll search the premises for any clues. I'll keep you updated on the progress." Vikram and Vinod exited the building.

Chapter 17

Re-investigate Arjun

Vikram and Vinod arrived at the hospital, exhausted from a long day. It was already 10 p.m., and two patients were still patiently waiting to see a doctor. As they entered the busy hospital, Vikram took out his phone and dialled Dr. Manisha's number.

"I still have two patients I need to see. You can continue with the investigation, and I'll join you once I've finished with the consultations," Dr. Manisha informed Vikram over the phone.

Both Vikram and Vinod entered Arjun's Room to find Arjun engrossed in conversation with his dad. Curious, Vikram asked, "What are dad and son talking about?" as they walked in together. Arjun's father stood up from his chair and replied, "Nothing, sir. We were just discussing how early treatment by the doctor saved his life."

Vikram turned to Arjun after getting approval from his father and asked, "Mind if I continue with my question?" Arjun shook his head, and Vikram proceeded to introduce Vinod to Arjun and his dad.

"You mentioned that after taking the injection, it made you feel active and full of energy," Vikram inquired. Arjun nodded in agreement. "Everything was going fine until a week later when I started experiencing headaches," Arjun shared.

"When I went back to see Dr. Prasad, he reassured us and prescribed some pills and another injection. The headache disappeared after that." "But after a week, I developed a fever and rashes on my skin again.

The symptoms would go away on their own when I took medicine. That's when I requested my dad not to take me back to Dr. Prasad because he only gave injections and never checked on me or asked about what happened," Arjun explained to Vikram.

"He prescribed the medication assuming that I would have a fever and headache," he added. Meanwhile, Manisha entered the room and attentively listened to Arjun's account.

"So, I asked my father if we could visit another competent doctor in the city," Arjun mentioned. "My dad inquired about a good hospital in the area and eventually took me to Getwell Hospital."

Vikram followed up, "Did you inform Doctor Manisha about the supplement injection?" Arjun revealed, "Sir, I wasn't aware of the name of the injection or whether any prescriptions were given. I also didn't know if it had any connection to the injection I received."

Arjun interjected, "At that point, I explained to the doctor that I had received a vitamin injection a month prior." Dr. Manisha informed Vikram, "Sir, Arjun had a fever and rashes all over his body," as she received and handed him his file. "That's why I prescribed medication for the fever and rashes. I also advised him to return if his condition didn't improve."

"Today, he returned to the hospital with a fever, stomach pain, and a severe headache," Dr. Manisha shared. "Knowing about Divya's situation, I recommended an advanced blood test. The results showed a very small amount of antinode, which counteracts the harmful effects of the previous medication."

Vikram expressed his gratitude, saying, "Arjun, thank you for your cooperation. Take it easy and get well soon. Don't worry; you are safe. I'll see you soon. Good night."

Vinod and Vikram left Arjun's room and patiently awaited Dr. Manisha. She checked on Arjun and gave instructions to the nurse on duty before joining the police officers outside.

"This is no ordinary case," Vikram confided in Dr. Manisha. "It appears to be a medical scam. I need to locate Dr. Prasad to uncover the truth."

Vikram urgently conveyed to the doctor, "We've already seen two patients, but we don't know how many more are affected. We need to crack this case immediately."

Arjun's dad interrupted their conversation and anxiously asked Vikram, "Sir, why are you investigating? Is my son, okay?" Vinod reassured him, "Sir, your son is no longer in danger. Please don't panic."

when Dr. Manisha shared her findings, Dr. Manisha solemnly explained, "Dr. Prasad didn't administer a simple vitamin injection to Arjun. He administered a powerful drug that contains a mixture of potent chemicals, not suitable for regular individuals, especially minors. Such medicines require careful handling under a doctor's supervision."

Arjun's dad was stunned and overwhelmed, grabbing onto Vinod for support. Vikram assured him, "Don't worry. Arjun is safe. We will track down the person responsible for this medical scam."

Instructing Arjun's dad to keep this information confidential to avoid jeopardizing the investigation, Vikram added, "Unfortunately, a 17-year-old girl who received the same drug is now in a coma, being treated in the ICCU unit of the same hospital."

Arjun's dad expressed his gratitude to Dr. Manisha and Vikram and shared, "Dr. Prasad has two close friends, Babu and Kumar, who often gather at his house. I hope this information helps your investigation."

Glancing at the time, which showed 11:15 p.m., Vinod proposed going to Ramesh's house. Vikram informed Dr. Manisha, "Alright, doctor. I will take the morning off tomorrow and return. For now, I need to head to the investigation cell based on suspicions. We have arrested Ramesh."

Dr. Manisha empathetically said, "Oh, I see. That's great news. You must be exhausted after a long day. It's already 11:30 p.m. Did you manage to have dinner?" Vikram assured her, "We ate something on the way to keep our energy up. "

"But doctor, I'm not just tired, I feel a sense of urgency. If we hadn't taken action, who knows how many people would have fallen victim to this scam?"

Vikram, joined by Vinod, sincerely expressed their gratitude, "On behalf of myself, Vinod, and our team, thank you for the timely information you provided." She smiled and added, "Let's hope our team swiftly identifies the culprit and takes the necessary actions."

Dr. Manisha continued, "I will be staying at the hospital tonight to monitor Divya and Arjun's health. Please don't hesitate to reach out if you need further assistance." Vikram thanked the doctor and, along with Vinod, left the hospital around 11:30 p.m.

Vikram instructed Vinod to take him to Ramesh's house and contacted Subhash to inquire about the developments at work. Subhash informed him, "Sir, I managed to obtain the laptop password from Ramesh. I will access the laptop and search for any valuable clues. Have you arrived at his house?" Vikram replied, "We just finished investigating Arjun at Getwell Hospital, and now we are heading to Ramesh's house."

Chapter 18

Search at Ramesh's House

A little after midnight, the Innova drove back into the quiet Sunshine Colony neighbourhood. It stopped on the side of the road, not too far from Ramesh's house. Vikram and Vinod got out of the car and walked toward Ramesh's house.

One of the police constables ran over to open the gate as Vikram and Vinod approached it. He put up a salute when he saw Vikram. The other police constable gave Vikram and Vinod an extra bow as they got closer to him.

Both cops were dressed in their normal clothes. Because of this, no one in society knew about the security and Ramesh's arrest. The two of them were excited to see what Vikram would inform them.

"Have you finished dinner?" Vikram asked.

"Yes, Subhash sir arranged dinner for us," the constable replied.

"Did anyone come here looking for Ramesh?" Then Vikram asked.

"Sir, at 8 p.m., three boys in their teens came to me and inquired about Ramesh," the cop said. They even asked us who we were and why we were waiting outside the house.

"It must be Kunal and his friends," Vinod thought. How did you answer them then?"

"We told him we were distant relatives waiting for him," Constable said. "The three boys talked amongst themselves before leaving."

"One hour before, at 10:45 p.m., a Hyundai Creta came and halted near the gate, and I tried to reach it, but it flew away," said a different policeman. "But I took note of the car number and sent it on to Subhash, sir."

Vikram likes both of the constables. They were told to open the door. They both went into the house.

There was a big table with books and papers on it on the left side of the room. There were small pictures of kids all over the walls. Vinod said, "This must be his classroom."

The door to the room across the hall was left closed. Vinod opened the door. Both entered the room; on the table, there were written papers, files, an external hard drive, and a computer. Vinod said, "This has to be his office."

As Vikram looked at the files, he saw that one of them was called "Mission Memory Enhancers," and below it was the names Ramesh Babu, Venkat Prasad, and Ram Kumar.

"I was shocked," so Vikram called Vinod and gave him the file, saying, "Vinod, please look over this." Even Vinod was shocked and said, "Sir Ramesh Babu is one person!"

Turning around, Vinod called Vikram while pointing to the wall across from him. There was a picture of three guys together on the wall.

It was about 1:30 in the morning when Subhash called Vinod. When Vinod picked up the phone, he said, "Hi Vinod, put the call on speaker. I want to talk to you both."

"Hi!" Vikram said. "Sir, I saw some very shocking things on this laptop," Subhash said. That's when Vikram spoke up and said,

"Mission Memory Enhancers."

"Subhash, we are also looking at the same file," Vinod replied. We'll talk about it more after we reach the office." The call ended.

Vikram and Vinod quickly looked over the papers. Their eyes got really big, and they looked shocked as they turned the pages.

As it was an emergency Vikram called the commissioner, "Sir, Sorry to disturb you in these late hours. We have found shocking details here at Ramesh's residence. Sir, if you could come to the investigation office, we will show you the important details." The commissioner agreed and said he would be right there in the investigation office in a moment.

Furthermore, Vinod phoned Dr. Manisha and asked, "Madam, sorry to disturb you, can you come to the office? We have recovered a few files. We need your help to know about the medical terms and the names of medications in the file. Dr. Manisha agreed and said she would come to the investigation office.

Vinod called Subhash, "We have completed the search work at Ramesh's residence and are leaving for our office. The Commissioner, Sir, and Dr. Manisha are also on their way. to discuss the findings."

Subhash made a note of the information shared, and he called the constables and informed them too.

Vinod drove his vehicle fast, and on their way to the office, Vikram made a call to Inspector Sunil. "Sunil, what is the status?" asked Vikram. "Did you get to meet Dr. Prasad?"

Sunil answered, "Sir, I was going to call you. He isn't at the office or home yet. I took the cell phone from his wife and put her under house arrest with two female police constables. Three police officers and I are waiting outside for Dr. Prasad to arrive."

Vikram spoke in a faster tone, "Sunil, I had sent you a picture of three men. The person in the blue shirt is Venkat Prasad. Ramesh Babu is next, and Ram Kumar is last. We have arrested Ramesh Babu and are in search of Venkat Prasad and Ram Kumar."

He further continued, "Sunil, I want them arrested. They should leave the city. try to find them."

Sunil hung up the phone and put an end to the talk. Then he went inside Prasad's house to question his wife, Nirmala. Nirmala had no clue about Prasad.

Vikram and Vinod with all the files, hard drives, and pictures, were traveling to the investigation office.

Chapter 19

The Shocking Revelation

At 2:30 a.m., Vikram and Vinod entered the investigation's office. Vikram made his way straight to the room where Ramesh was being held. He told Subhash to open his door.

After walking in, he saw that Ramesh was tied to the chair's handle. According to Ramesh, he was sitting comfortably and eating the whole meal that was brought to him. Ramesh tried to look calm.

"Hi, Mr. Babu, how're things going?" Vikram said it with a bit of sarcasm to show how angry he was at that moment. I hope you enjoyed our service. Where are you on your mission with the Memory Enhancers?" Asked Vikram.

A 1000-volt electric shock happened to Ramesh. He felt he got stuck. However, he kept his cool and didn't show that he was nervous. Ramesh didn't answer the question that was right in front of him.

Vinod stated in anger, "Sir, this morning in the hospital, he was shouting at Divya's parents because they said Divya got a headache after coming from his class. He made the hospital such a dramatized place, and they must have trusted him so much that they sent their daughter to his classes."

Subhash continued, "Sir, I was shocked when I read his research paper. What the heck are these people doing, messing up the lives of teens?"

"You can't be quiet for long," Vinod told Ramesh. "You will speak up."

"Sunil where are you now?" asked Vikram. He said, "Sir, I got the address of RK Pharmaceutical; it's in the industrial estate area; within 20 minutes, we will reach there."

"Sunil," Vikram said. "Both Prasad and Kumar need to be arrested immediately and presented for investigations. Send police officers in different directions to look for them." Giving the phone to Subhash, Vikram told him to let Sunil know what was going on.

Vikram drew a chair and sat down in front of him with a picture in his hand. Three happy people are holding a file called "Mission Memory Enhancers." After that, he set the file called "memory enhancers" on the table. His question was, "What is this, Ramesh Babu?"

"Do you have a name other than Ramesh Babu?" Immediately tell me more about these "Memory Enhancers." angrily shouted Vikram.

Without saying anything, Ramesh stayed quiet. Vikram warned Ramesh that if he didn't speak up, things would change for him.

Turning around, Vikram saw Vinod. Vinod flipped a switch, and Subhash turned a knob. Eventually, Ramesh could feel an electric current running through his body. A scream came from him. Subhash turned off and said this was pretty basic.

"I saw many kids' and teenage children's photos on the walls of your dining room," said Vikram. "It's amazing how much they believed you. But you've broken their trust."

Vikram became very angry and asked in a rude way, "What did that girl Divya do to you? At the hospital, did you see her? She is in a coma. Is it a crime for her to believe that you are also one who has gone to help make the future better?"

"Now tell me what 'Memory Enhancers' are; come on, speak out," said Vikram.

In pain, Ramesh yells as Vinod applies an electric current to the metal chair where he is sitting again, but this time for a little longer. Then Ramesh said, "I'll talk about Memory Enhancers."

Ramesh asked for water. He was moved to a wooden chair, where Subhash tied him down tightly and gave him water. Vinod got ready to record his confession.

Ramesh started to talk. "Mission Memory Enhancers" is the project's name, and it's about making medicine that will help enhance the memory power of teenagers. We are all a part of this project, Dr. Prasad, myself, and Kumar."

"Only you three?" Vikram asked. "This record shows a connection between the two countries. Have you lost your mind? You are a man with a lot of education and a PhD. You are not wise about how to conduct research. Does this look like some kind of cooking contest?" shouted Vikram.

"Have you received permission to conduct these clinical trials?" he asked. "Are you familiar with the trial procedure?"

"What you three are doing is against the law," Vikram said. "You have no right to get involved in the lives of teenagers. It's only Divya and Arjun who are affected. How many trials have you conducted?"

Ramesh said, "We're researching for an international medical forum. There, my friend got permission, and it will soon be for sale on the foreign market. So, he has followed the rules set by other countries. He took care of everything."

"My job is simply to invent the medicine," Ramesh said". The medicine doesn't have many drugs, and they won't hurt the patient. I also made an antidote medicine to offset the effects of the memory booster drug on the body."

"We would have then gone to London to show the medicine and get it approved. They only need five trials of the drug to go well. The fifth attempt, on Divya, failed. If it had succeeded, we would have flown out of India and become famous all over the world," said Ramesh.

Vinod, Subhash, and Vikram were taken aback upon hearing what Ramesh was saying, and they were motionless for that moment. A knock on the door was heard. A constable was standing outside when Subhash opened the door. He then said, "Sir, Commissioner Sir, and Dr. Manisha Madam had come."

After locking the door to Ramesh's room, they went into the office. Dr. Manisha and the commissioner of police were waiting for them. Everyone there gave the commissioner a salute.

Observing them "You people didn't take a break?" Dr. Manisha asked. Vikram expressed, "Doctor, already we are worried; now which teenager is going to get injected?"

The commissioner said, "It looks like this case is very sensitive. If not, you wouldn't have called me at this time."

"These three have made a medicine that will enhance brain power," Vikram said, putting the picture and file on the table.

Further, he continued, "They used five teenagers as test subjects for medical studies. Divya was the last trail, but it didn't work. The finishing trail can be done whenever they want, or it has to be done. Inspector Sunil and his team have been sent to find Prasad and Kumar."

Subhash got Ramesh's laptop out and showed Dr. Manisha the results of the study. "I can't guess what it is," she said, adding, "The few chemical names given are medicines that are very dangerous."

Vikram revealed what Ramesh had told him to both of them. "We need to get details about the London Medical Council mentioned in the document," Vikram said. "There is a list of some people from whom they got this project," said Vikram.

Amidst the talk, the commissioner stated, "First, I have to tell the higher officials about this scam. Do not worry, I can get the information about the international medical forum from the medical council; just give me a copy of the documents."

"Vikram, Vinod, Subhash, Sunil, and all the other constables did a great job," said the commissioner of police.

The commissioner and Dr. Manisha left. Vikram asked Subhash, "Did you get the names and contact information of other teenagers who were given the medicine?"

Chapter 20

The Final Trail

Kumar went into his office at 2:30 a.m. and told his security guards not to let anyone in. He then drove his car behind his office and parked it there.

He walked into the office and then to his office room. Dr. Prasad was in his office holding a conference call with people from other countries, and the call was going on for a while.

When the call ended, Prasad asked Kumar, "Have you set up a teen?" "Will it be a boy or a girl?"

Kumar replied, "Yes, it's a girl. She's the daughter of one of my maintenance workers. He was worried about her health because she was weak. This will help us in our final trial."

"With whom were you doing the conference call?" Kumar asked Prasad a question.

"To Mr. Mike, I requested that he set up a meeting with the chief within the next 15 days so that we can present the document on time and obtain authorization," said Prasad.

But we had to leave this place right away when the trail was over. This place is not safe," warned Prasad.

Kumar asked, "We both? What about Babu? Do you know

anything else about him?"

According to Prasad, "I doubt he's in police custody. My driver saw two police officers at his home when he went to get the documents. This is why I want to finish this final trail as soon as possible."

"When will the girl come?" Prasad asked. Kumar replied, "She will arrive after 7 a.m. I can't call her at this time."

Prasad said, "Ramesh messed up when he injected Divya." "We've decided not to perform trials on known teenagers. He is making us suffer."

He didn't know that Prasad was the one who gave Divya the shot at Ramesh's house. Prasad assumes that he would have left India before Kumar knew about it.

Prasad keeps venting, "My dream is to make more money and live a fancy life. But Babu has made things hard. He didn't want to work on this research very much. He probed me about a lot of things. It was my mistake to include him in this project."

Kumar said, "Babu, he is our friend. We have known each other since we were children."

Prasad said, "He always thinks of me as a competitor for him." Prasad had told.

Negatively to Kumar about Babu. Now Kumar was in a confused state of mind.

Prasad continued to brainwash Kumar: "Kumar, you have to identify whether you want fame and fortune or make over-the-counter medicines in your pharmaceutical company."

When there was some silence, Kumar spoke up. "Prasad, let's finish the last trail successfully and leave this place, and I am always with you."

"Kumar," Prasad said. I promise I'll never let you down. I'm just waiting for 7 a.m. to come around. It's best if the girl comes early. After that, we can finish the trail."

Kumar asked, "Do we need to go to Babu's house after the clinical trial is over tomorrow morning because Babu has all the records and paperwork?" Prasad said, "No need. I have soft copies of all documents. It's risky to go to his place right now."

Prasad also said, "If he is caught by the police, by now he will tell them everything about the project." He can't take pain for him. Let's go out of the city after the trial. He doesn't know that we're about to finish the last trial."

There was a lot they wanted to do on their last trail before the day ended, but they didn't know what was in store for them the next day.

Meanwhile, around 3:30 a.m., Inspector Sunil and two police officers arrived at RK Pharmaceuticals, which is outside of the city.

The Security guard standing at the gate said the business was closed, so they should be back by 9 a.m. the next day.

Kumar screamed in the office, "Oh no, police! Prasad, come with me! We need to leave this place!"

Dragging Prasad to the back door, he went in. Both of them got into the car that was parked in the garden and drove away through the back gate.

"Sir," the constable shouted, Sunil saw a car exiting through the back gate, "they got away through the back gate." Said the constable.

Sunil and the police constables got on and sped off toward Kumar's car.

The police car was going quickly so they wouldn't miss the suspect. Kumar took the street to get around the traffic. It wasn't long before the police car arrived.

Kumar's car went from the street to the road. The police vehicle driver looked at the road for traffic and saw the road was clear and fine. He sped up his car, went around Kumar's, pulled up in front of it, and hit the brakes hard. Kumar slammed on the brakes and stopped the car completely to avoid a crash.

Sunil and the officer in the police van went to the car and picked up Prasad and Kumar there. They were handcuffed right away and taken to the police car. Sunil told a police constable to drive their car to the investigation office.

When Inspector Sunil called Vikram, he told him that Prasad and Kumar had been caught and that he would be at the investigation office in fifteen minutes.

Chapter 21

Meet with DGP

Around 5:30 a.m., Sunil, Prasad, and Kumar showed up at the investigation office. Each of them was put in a room by itself. Later, Sunil went up to Vikram, posted a salute to him, and started to explain what had happened.

"Sir, when we entered the company, they fled through the back gate," said Sunil. But we chased and caught them. As it was early hours of morning, there was no traffic or people on the roads so we could catch them easily."

Vikram said, "Well done, Sunil and team." He gathered together the inspectors and constables who were in charge of this case. "Congratulations and thanks to my outstanding police team. Without your help, we wouldn't have made it this far. It's time to keep the facts of this case secret. This information shouldn't get to the public. Remember to keep an eye cut for the media to get this information," said Vikram.

The Commissioner of Police called Vikram on the phone. In response, Vikram asked, "Sir, have you received the information about the London Medical Forum?"

"To go any further, we need our DGP's permission," the commissioner said. I called him and told him about the scam.

Immediately, he called me over to his house to discuss. I told him everything in detail, and he permitted me to move forward.

"He also told the Home Minister's secretary about it. DGP sir has also asked for help from other countries to look into the medical forum."

"Thank you," Vikram said, "now we're going to question three of them." that they show up in court at 10 a.m. and be behind the bars.

Vikram told his inspectors to bring all three of them and the caretaker, Raju, into the same room. Vikram told all the constables to be careful and not let anyone in.

Vikram went to the room where the investigation was going to happen.

Chapter 22

The Trios Statement

Venkat Prasad, Ramesh Babu, and Ram Kumar were blindfolded and tied to the chair when Vikram walked in, except for the caretaker, Raju.

Vikram pulled up a chair and sat in the middle of the room. Vinod began to record their sayings on the video recorder. The two other inspectors were behind them.

Vikram asked Raju a question: "How many years have you been working at Ramesh's house?" Have you seen his friends at Ramesh's house?"

"Sir, I've been working for Ramesh sir for the past three years," said Raju.

"I do all the work at Ramesh sir's house. Only a few times have Prasad sir and Kumar sir been to Ramesh sir's house. Whenever both sirs come to Ramesh sir's house, he tells me to go for a movie or enjoy dinner outside. Sir, give me money to go out and enjoy. Consequently, I go for a movie and eat out."

Vikram told Vinod to put him back in his room and lock those doors. Raju and Vinod left the room.

"So, how did the idea of 'Mission Memory Enhancers' start?" asked Vikram.

Vikram turned to Ramesh and asked, "I hope you can shed some light on this."

Ramesh stated, "A year ago, Dr. Prasad and a few other doctors from the state had the opportunity to attend a medical conference in London," At that meeting, a doctor was praised for making a new drug.

Ramesh continued, "After returning from that conference, he invited us to his house for dinner and said that we should join together and invent a medicine."

"Why did you decide to make a medicine?" Vikram asked Dr. Prasad. "Is there any reason to?"

There was no response from Dr. Prasad. He screams in surprise all of a sudden. because within his chair, Vinod applied a small amount of electricity.

"Is this current sufficient, or do you require more?" Vinod asked. It would be great if you could help us out.

"At the conference dinner party, I met the doctor who was honored for his invention," Prasad mentioned. We talked about his study and how he did it. I told myself it wouldn't be easy to get to this level of fame. "Excuse me," a person behind me said at the time.

"A white complexation with cat eyes and golden hair man smiled at me and introduced himself, 'I am Dr. Mike'." I said hello and said, "My name is Dr." He finished, "Prasad."

Mike said, "Hello Prasad, I saw that you were asking about how he made a new drug, etc. You are aware that it requires a lot of time, and money, and abides by many laws and regulations. Meet me tomorrow at 1 p.m. at Well Street Pizza if you know about it."

Vikram asked Prasad, "So you met him?" "How come you believe a stranger in these sensitive matters, and creating medicine is not a game?"

"I met him, and he introduced me to a small group of doctors, scientists, and research analysts," said Prasad.

"They all set up a medical forum where new medicines are made and sold, so there isn't a hard method to follow. But their community still needs to be signed up. They do, however, recognize skill and hard work."

"If I had finished the final trial successfully, I would have flown to London and sold the medical research paper for a good price." All of this is because of Divya and this Babu," Prasad said with anger.

Kumar says, "When the medical forum accepts the medicine, Prasad says he will get approval to make it in my pharmaceutical company and send it to another country. Babu, Babu, see what he's saying."

Vikram told Subhash to take off the blindfold.

Ramesh said, "Prasad, we didn't question you at all. We believed what you said and worked hard because of it. I called you more than once about the permission and process you said your friend had finished."

"Even though I knew you always put yourself first, I didn't think you'd be that self-centered. My trust in you had been broken," said Ramesh.

There was silence in the room for just a moment. "We're not interested in your emotional discussions," said Vikram. "Okay, you damn it. Firstly, tell me which five teens you gave the injection to. Any information about their health after the medicine was given to them?" asked Vikram.

Kumar said, "Sir Arjun was our first trial person. Then, we set up a medical camp in an ashram with the help of an NGO. There, three girls were given injections.".

Then Subhash asked, "Ashram children? Exactly why are you people being so mean? Some people lack kindness. He asked sarcastically why there were only three teens. There are lots of teenagers in the ashram; you could have completed the entire trail there itself." Subhash was full of anger when he expressed these words.

Vikram went up to Ramesh Babu and sat down in front of him. He asked, how did you trap that innocent girl, Divya?"

Chapter 23

Ramesh's Confession

Vikram sat down next to Ramesh Babu and asked, "How did you trap that innocent girl?"

Ramesh did not say anything and kept his head down. As Vikram lifted his head, Ramesh saw that Vikram's eyes were red with anger.

Ramesh started to say, "On Friday evening, by 5:30 p.m., Divya came to my house to return a reference book. She was hoping." I asked her what happened.

"Divya said a bike came from the opposite direction; she was riding her bicycle back from NEET class and jumped off to avoid a crash," said Ramesh.

Ramesh added, "I told her she needed to get a tetanus injection because she fell on the road."

She said that she would go with her father to Getwell Hospital and get the tetanus injection done. But I told Prasad, and he came over with the injection right away.

Kumar was shocked to learn that Prasad knew about the trial. He told lies when he said he didn't know.

"I convinced her that my friend would come home and inject her." That being said, she wasn't ready and said she would tell her parents. It was hard for me to persuade her.

Prasad came over and filled the tetanus medicine in the syringe in front of her while showing her how to properly give it. She closed her eyes and turned to the other side when he went to give the injection. At that moment, Prasad changed the syringe that had our booster medicine and gave her the injection.

"How dare you do that to the girl?" Vikram asked Ramesh as he hit the table hard. She thought you would never hurt her. However, you were a rude man."

"I'll put you all behind bars for the rest of your life. You all act like such jerks. "A doctor, scholar, and pharmacist," said Vikram.

"You all never knew the value of life." Vikram then left the room. The inspector locked them in their separate rooms.

It was seven in the morning. Vikram asked a constable to get tea for everyone. To show the case in court, Vinod was writing about it. Sunil and Subhash were helping him write the case history.

Vikram made a call to the commissioner and explained the investigation. Further, he asked whether he could get in touch with the London cops.

"Sir," called a constable to Vikram, "look at this news on the TV." Everyone was looking at the video of Prasad and Kumar's arrest on the highway.

The reporter said, "Last night, police seized a car and arrested two people inside, who are they? Is it possible that they are terrorists? Or any criminal who is dressed like a police officer? We need to find the police car and the black car." This news was broadcast as flash news on all news channels.

The news on the channel continues: "As it was recorded from a long distance, the vehicle is not visible, it said. We're trying to get in touch with higher-up police officers to find out if this is an arrest or a kidnapping.?"

Vikram asked Sunil, "Where are your car and Kumar's car?" Sunil said, "Our police car is parked in our underground park area. and Kumar's car is parked with other cars behind the office."

Vikram answered, "I think we shouldn't focus on this. Within a few hours, we have to produce all four in court for the case hearing." "Sir, after the court judgment, we will tell them what happened," said Vinod, and others agreed with him.

"Sir, good morning." Vinod got a call from the police commissioner.

The commissioner said, "I'd like to talk to Vikram."

Vinod said, "Just a moment, I will give it to Vikram, sir."

Vinod handed Vikram the phone and said, "The commissioner is on the line."

The commissioner told Vikram, "I do believe you have seen the news channel."

Vikram said, you're right, sir—we chose not to stress on the news. The most important thing is to produce them before the law and know what the final judgment will be for the three friends.

The commissioner said, "Few reports have visited our DIG and asked for action on the matter; DIG Sir has said that he will find them and answer them by this afternoon." After sharing the information with Vikram, the Commissioner hung up the phone.

Vikram asked Vinod, "Are the FIRs ready? Are all the documents ready? and we are going to court in about 30 minutes. The commissioner said the first hearing of the case will be held behind closed doors."

"Good morning, madam," Vikram greeted Dr. Manisha. She wished him well in return and said, "Sir, your voice sounds demanding. I hope you've solved the case."

"Again, thanks to you, ma'am, we are going to produce them in court today at 10 a.m.," said Vikram. Would you be able to make it to court at 10 a.m.? Because your report is the first FIR in this case."

The doctor replied, "Yes, sure, Vikram sir. I will be there at 10 a.m.

Vikram asked the doctor, "Don't tell anyone about this right now." When the case goes to a public hearing, we can let Divya's parents and other people know."

Dr. Manisha asked Vikram, "Sir, the breaking news flashing on TV is the arrest related to this case."

Vikram said, "Yes, ma'am, we are not focusing on it right now. We might get in touch with the press to let them know after the case gets registered and the hearing starts in court." They finished their talk and went back to work.

At 9 a.m., a police vehicle drove up, and the four suspects—Ramesh Babu, Prasad, Kumar, and caretaker Raju—and two inspectors—Subhash, Sunil, and constables—got inside the police van.

The Innova was following the police vehicle, and Vinod and Vikram were driving it. They were both on their way to court. The DIG and the Commissioner of Police are also on their way to court. Dr. Manisha also showed up at court.

Chapter 24

Judgement Day

At 9:45 a.m., the police showed up at the session court in their police van and Innova.

Dr. Manisha arrived at the court.

The news writers are interested in what's going on. There was a story going around, so when they saw Vikram, they surrounded him and questioned him.

Vikram replied, "I will answer all about the cases after meeting the judge."

The DIG and Police Commissioner arrived in different cars five minutes later and went into the courtroom.

The cop and Dr. Manisha went into court with the suspects.

At the request of the police, two judges handled the case in a private room.

The case background was produced for the judges. After that, the judges asked the public prosecutor to explain the case. The public prosecutor called Vikram and asked him to brief Using what Dr. Manisha had said to him, Vikram began to tell the story of the case.

The three inspectors were showing the proof of documents to the judges while Vikram was telling them about the case. They also produced the audio and video recordings from the probe.

The judges called the commissioner and allowed him to talk about the case. The commissioner said, "Honourable Judges, on enquiring with the London Police, we came to know that the medical forum for which Dr. Prasad has made this toxic medicine is an unauthorized medical forum; they do not have a license." The London cops are looking into the forum to see if it has anything to do with terrorism.

The judges said they should go to jail, and the hearing for their case will start the next day. They insisted that the police produce the witness and the proof at the next hearing. For those who are suspected of a crime, "the court will punish them.

Before taking the suspects to the police vehicle and then to jail, inspectors covered their faces.

According to Vikram, the news conference was set for 3 p.m. at their investigation office. Vikram, his inspectors, and his constables showed up in front of the press at 3 p.m.

Vikram said, "I'd like to get right to the point. This morning, a video of two people being arrested went viral on a news station. Yes, our officer in the early morning hours was able to catch two people who were involved in a medical scam. Three people have been arrested in this case; all of them have ties with an international country.".

Vinod told the press, "They were preparing medicine illegally and conducting clinical trials. We have therefore arrested them. Tomorrow is the first day of the hearing. From tomorrow, you can start keeping up with the case."

Reporters took pictures of Vikram and his crew. All the news stations showed it as breaking news, and all the major newspapers ran it with big headlines.

The trial started the next day. It started with Dr. Manisha and then moved on to Divya's parents, friends, and other people she knew who were involved in the investigation.

The police commissioner showed the judge a video clip from Mr. George, a special police officer in London. The judge told the courtroom security staff to play the video.

The video greeting starts, "Good day to the magistrate and the police officials. Thank you to Vikram and his police officials for helping me and sharing information about the medical mafia group. My name is George, and I am the Superintendent of London Police. They were someone we were looking for. They are linked to the terrorist group, and I promised that we would find them, put them in jail right away, and maintain the safety of teens."

The judges gave all three convicts life sentences in prison after hearing the proof. The licenses of both Dr. Prasad and Kumar Pharmaceutical were taken away.

Unfortunately, Ramesh can't go to college or university to take classes. Ramesh Babu cried when he heard the final verdict.

The judges added, "Considering the employees of RK Pharmaceutical, the government will take over the company. His family will be able to live off of 20% of the company's income."

The judges said, "Ramesh, Prasad, and Kumar all three have to take responsibility for the treatment cost of all the five children to whom they have done the clinical trials."

"As the caretaker is innocent and was not involved in the guilty activity," the verdict explains. The court let him go, and Ramesh was told to pay him Rs 5 lakhs to make up for the stress and trouble he caused in his life.

The judges said the case against Mission Memory Enhancers is over.

The DIG and the commissioner of police, "Congratulations, Vikram, Vinod, Subash, Sunil, and the constables; you all did an outstanding job, and the entire nation is proud of you. Your actions saved the lives of many teens."

Many people thanked Vikram, Vinod, Subhash, Sunil, and the police constables who worked hard to solve the case and sent their best wishes.

People also thanked and met Dr. Manisha on TV.

People prayed for Divya to come out of a coma. Within a few months, George and his team found the medical mafia gang and put them in jail.

Chapter 25

Congratulations & Celebrations

Once Vikram was done telling the whole story of how they destroyed the "Mission Memory Enhancer," there was silence in the commissioner's office conference room.

As the police commissioner walked into the room, loud cheering could be heard from behind him from Vinod, Subhash, Sunil, the constables, Dr. Manisha, Dr. Sandeep, Sudhir, Shylaja, Jaspal, Veena, Arjun, and Arjun's father.

Sudhir and Shylaja thanked Vikram, his team, and Dr. Manisha for saving their daughter. They are sure that Dr. Manisha will help their daughter get back to normal.

Kunal, Anu, Charan, and Pradeep brought Divya over in a wheelchair into the conference hall. There was silence in the meeting place for a short time.

Kunal and friends said they would stand by their friend Divya forever. They will help her recover from her illness. They all bowed down and thanked Vikram and his team.

Yes.... Let's hope Divya wakes up and goes back to her dream life.

We also want to thank Vikram Sir and his team for this amazing operation and the many children whose lives they have saved.

Acknowledgements

Throughout my life, I have been thankful to the Almighty. I am grateful to my readers who choose to read my book and it will be a part of my achievement.

I am grateful to my dear spouse Renga and my gorgeous daughters Krushali and Hithali for motivating me and for their unwavering belief in me.

Thank you for your blessings and prayers, my parents and in-laws.

Big thanks to the Mugafi Community for guiding me through this writing journey and assisting me in establishing my writing career.

Heartfelt thanks to Inkfeathers for enthusiastically publishing my narrative and making my book available worldwide.

Sujatha Renganathan is a freelance career counsellor based in Navi Mumbai. She completed her schooling in Chennai as a science graduate and as a diploma student. She was a computer programmer and a teacher.

However, she discovered happiness and fulfillment in her passion for creativity, which inspired her to express herself through words and digital creations. Her writing adventure began with poems, and she has produced a book titled "Poetic Lounge." This is her first novel.

You can connect with her at icebergunplugged@gmail.com.

INKFEATHERS
PUBLISHING

www.inkfeathers.com

We love creating beautiful books for you!

Be a part of our ever-growing community of authors.
Grow, write, and publish with us!

Connect with us on socials.
We'd love to hear from you!

@InkfeathersPublishing

www.ingramcontent.com/pod-product-compliance
Lightning Source LLC
Chambersburg PA
CBHW021020160726
47994CB00006B/2597